#11

DANCING WITH DANGER IN LAS VEGAS

A HUMOROUS TIFFANY BLACK MYSTERY

A. R. WINTERS

COPYRIGHT

JOIN THE AR WINTERS NEWSLETTER

～

Find out about the latest releases by AR Winters,
and get access to exclusive free copies of her books:

Click Here To Join

You can also follow AR Winters on Facebook

DANCING WITH DANGER IN LAS VEGAS
(A TIFFANY BLACK STORY)

∼

When Tiffany Black is asked to look into the mysterious death of a young lawyer, she finds herself uncovering all kinds of legal conundrums.

Meanwhile, Ian declares himself bored with life, and with Nanna as his accomplice, embarks on an unwise adventure.

my casino job and be an investigator full-time, but PI business tends to ebb and flow and probably wouldn't pay all my bills.

The casino pit has become my second home now, with its loud, garish carpets, bright overhead lights, and the constant jingle of the slot machines.

I dealt a few more hands before I felt the tap on my shoulder. When I turned around, I smiled and saw that it was Nancy, my replacement dealer. I murmured a polite farewell to the players still sitting at my table, clapped my hands out before me, and threaded my way out of the pit.

A few minutes later, I'd changed out of my red-and-black dealer's uniform and was stepping out into the slightly chilly Vegas morning. It was time to head back to my apartment and face the day—or more specifically, the client who'd called me yesterday afternoon, begging to meet me as soon as possible.

I barely had time to rush home, wash off my makeup and take a quick shower before my neighbor Ian showed up.

Ian is like an overenthusiastic puppy, with his bright, eager green eyes and shocking curly red hair. I met him while on the run from a maniac with a knife, and these days, he helps me out on my cases.

At first, his naivety and incredible optimism annoyed me, but over time, I've come to appreciate his loyalty and his big heart. These days, I think of him as the slightly annoying younger brother I never had.

Ian lives across the hall from me. His apartment is a mirror image of my own modest one-bedroom: the front door opens to a living-dining area flanked by a kitchenette, and a door leads to a bedroom and bathroom.

Both our apartments are furnished with cheap discount-store furniture, but I tend to make sure mine is relatively neat and clean. Ian's place looks and smells like a college dorm room, and the cleanest item in his place is his kitten Snowflake's scratching post.

Snowflake is a tiny white bundle of fur with bright blue eyes. Her personality is pretty much the opposite of Ian's; most of the time she's aloof and looks at us superciliously, but occasionally she deigns to let us scratch her ears and rub her belly.

Today, she decided to make herself at home on top of my fridge, and she licked her paws slowly and watched Ian and me.

While I was happy to see Snowflake again, I was happier still to see the large Tupperware box that Ian was carrying.

He placed it on my kitchen counter and opened the lid with a flourish. "Cupcakes, again!"

I grinned broadly, my tiredness from the shift disappearing. "Yum! Hazelnut?"

"Yup. I decided to perfect them before moving on to a different flavor."

"I'm so glad you're baking again. You know I'd help, but I'm always so busy with the casino and these cases..."

"I know, I know," said Ian as I found two plates for us and quickly made some instant decaf coffee. I wanted real coffee, but I knew I needed to sleep soon. "But it's more fun when we're baking together. I found an amazing recipe for lemon cupcakes with lemon-buttercream frosting..."

"We'll make that one together," I promised him as we settled down on the couch and dug into the delicious cupcakes. They were perfect—rich and sweet and hazelnutty.

"How did Fiona convince you to meet her right after your shift?" said Ian.

"I'm not sure," I admitted. "I don't like meeting people right after work, but she said she really wanted to talk to me, and it was hard for her to make time around her job as an accountant."

"What's it about, anyway?"

"I don't know that either. But she sounded really desperate, and I guess I felt sorry for her."

We chewed our cupcakes silently for a few minutes, each lost in our own thoughts. I was thinking back to my most memorable cases. Sure, I've worked on a couple of easy surveillance jobs, but my first real case was looking into the death of casino owner Ethan Becker. Once I'd solved that case, word had spread that I was good at solving murders, and clients kept hiring me to look into suspicious deaths.

In many ways, I hate investigating murders: the crimes are tragic, and the perpetrators usually do a good job of covering up their tracks. And once a killer learns that I'm on their tail, they usually go all out to get me to stop investigating—including trying to kill me. It's no fun knowing that a murderer wants to make you his next victim.

But, on the other hand, these cases usually pay well. And along the way, I've become a bit of a softie who likes helping out other people. I like knowing that I've helped an innocent person get off the hook for a crime they didn't commit, and I like helping clients find closure when they're dealing with the death of a loved one.

Still, this wasn't really the life I'd expected when

I'd signed up to become a PI. I'd thought my days would be spent tailing cheating spouses, not piecing together clues to reveal a killer's identity.

Just as I finished my decaf, there was a knock on the door.

Ian and I looked at each other, and Snowflake jumped off the fridge and came over to us, ready to greet the visitor.

"Let's see what Fiona wants," said Ian, getting up slowly. "Whatever it is that's so urgent..."

2

Fiona Miller was a plump, petite woman who looked to be in her mid-forties. She had dark brown hair cut to just above her shoulders, and brown eyes with dark hollows under them.

She forced her thin lips into a smile as Ian and I introduced ourselves, and then she perched on the edge of a chair opposite the sofa.

"I really appreciate you meeting me like this," she murmured. "I know how hard it is to stay awake after a long shift."

Fiona was obviously stressed and on edge, and Ian looked like he felt as sorry for her as I did.

"Have a cupcake," he said, grabbing the Tupperware box and a plate. "They're delicious."

Fiona hesitated for a moment and then reached

forward and helped herself to a cupcake as I made three more mugs of steaming decaf.

"Thank you." She bit into the cupcake gingerly and chewed thoughtfully. "This really is delicious. Don't tell me you made it?"

Ian beamed and explained that he was getting interested in baking, just as Snowflake made her way over and rubbed up against Fiona's legs, hoping to be petted. Fiona obliged, scratching Snowflake between her ears, and Ian explained quickly how we'd rescued Snowflake from a horrible, mean woman.

I sat down on the sofa opposite Fiona, and the three of us sipped our decaf. I waited till Fiona had finished her cupcake and looked a great deal more relaxed before I said, "I know that my former client James told you about me, but what's this about?"

Fiona's dark eyes clouded over for a moment, and she gulped. There was a moment of stillness in the air. Finally, she said, "It's about my sister. Ella." There was another long pause; Snowflake realized Fiona had stopped petting her and strolled over to Ian.

Fiona cleared her throat and continued. "Ella died—was killed—two weeks ago. The police haven't gotten anywhere. I was told... I heard you can look into these things?"

She looked at me with pleading eyes and I gulped involuntarily. I hate making promises I can't keep, and I wasn't sure it would be a good idea to take on another murder case. The last murder I'd looked into, Ian and I had ended up facing the wrong end of a gun held by a killer, and I didn't want to repeat that scenario.

I said, "If the police haven't managed to find anything..."

"The police aren't really looking," said Fiona quickly. "They think it's a mugging gone wrong, but I know it's not."

"What makes you so sure?"

Fiona gestured with one hand. "They found her body near Balzar Avenue. I know that's a bad neighborhood, and muggings and shootings happen there, but Ella had no reason to go there. The cops don't care about murders in that neighborhood. They keep saying it's gang violence or a mugging, but I know it's not."

"How?" I repeated.

"I just know." Fiona frowned and tried to explain herself. "My sister was a lawyer. She had no reason to go near Balzar. And she's got a car, but she hadn't driven that day. They say she took a cab or got a lift, but there's no records of her getting a cab, and why would she get a lift over there? I talked to her earlier that night, and she told me she'd be staying in. She wanted to relax with a movie, so she skipped going to the office drinks that most of the associates had gone to."

I said, "It's still not very conclusive..."

Fiona looked from me to Ian and said, "What do you think?"

Ian looked at me helplessly. He has a bad habit of saying the wrong thing at the wrong time, so I've told him to let me do most of the talking when we deal with suspects or clients, but I knew that he was dying to take the case.

"I think Fiona's right," Ian said. "Why would Ella even go to Balzar?"

Deep in my gut, I sensed that Fiona was right, too. No one in their right mind would go to Balzar Avenue late at night, and something just felt off. But I didn't say that. I said, "Maybe there's something to it, but if the cops couldn't find anything unusual..."

"I don't think the cops really looked too hard," said Fiona. "They're short-staffed here in Vegas."

"But that doesn't mean I'll be able to find anything new," I said. "I don't want you to get your hopes up—even if it's strange that she went to Balzar late at night, it could still have just been a mugging gone wrong."

"I don't need guarantees," Fiona said. "I just need to know someone's really looked into it. The cops just wrote it off—at least I know you'll try harder. Even if you don't find out anything new."

Ian and I exchanged a glance, and I sipped my decaf thoughtfully. Fiona seemed quite reasonable, and it was probably a good idea to take this case. It might wind up being an easy one, and at the very least, it would keep me busy and stop me from worrying so much about what my friend Stone was up to.

"We'll do it," I said warily. "Let me go and get my standard PI contract, and then we can get started."

Fiona smiled, relieved. "Great. It'll be good to know the truth about what happened. Or at least part of the truth."

I forced myself to smile optimistically. The last murder I'd investigated was still fresh in my mind, as was the danger we'd faced. I hoped this case would be less dangerous.

3

Once the contracts were signed and Fiona wrote a check for my advance, I said, "We need to start at the beginning. I'll need to know everything about Ella—everything you can think of."

Fiona nodded. "I know. I told the cops everything I could think of, but there really wasn't too much."

Snowflake decided that she'd had enough human interaction for now and suddenly raced off for the fridge. She landed on top, settled down, and began to lick one paw meticulously.

The three of us watched her for a while, and then I turned back to Fiona. "What was Ella like?"

Fiona smiled. "I'm her sister, so obviously, I'm biased. But she was a great person. Really smart, really hardworking, conscientious. That's what made her such a great lawyer."

I wondered silently if those were also the qualities that had gotten her killed. "Where did she work?"

"Elman and Associates. She was just an associate, but she was doing well at work. Got lots of good projects, was up for a promotion. She was really happy with her job. The hours were long sometimes, but she didn't mind."

"How long was she working there?"

Fiona shrugged. "Ella moved to Vegas... what, two years ago? She moved here for the job. And I moved here a year later, to be closer to her. Our parents both died a few years back, and it was just the two of us."

I nodded and made a note. "Two years is long enough to meet lots of people."

"Ella wasn't that outgoing. Her closest friend, Felicity, was someone she went to law school with. Felicity works at a small law firm here."

I nodded. "Any other close friends?"

"No, Ella was too busy with work to socialize much. She hung out with the other associates sometimes. But she wasn't particularly close with anyone at work."

The strobe lights around the slot machine came to life suddenly, and a loud congratulatory tune blared out of the speakers hidden nearby.

The woman standing in front of the machine stared at it blankly, her mouth slightly ajar. The security guard closest to her was already making his way forward, and another nearby guard was talking into his mouthpiece furiously.

I let myself get distracted for a split second; I watched as realization slowly dawned on the woman's face, and her eyes lit up in a smile. I wasn't sure how much the jackpot had been, but I knew it was at least a half million dollars.

I enjoyed watching players win big at the Treasury Casino, but I didn't have the luxury of watching the whole scene unfold. I knew that the woman would be safely escorted to get her winnings, and her stay at the casino would be comped. She'd probably remember this night as one of the best nights of her life, but for me, this was just another night on the job.

I turned back to the blackjack players sitting opposite me and dealt out another hand. The three men all wore serious expressions, and they were so intent on their game that they probably didn't even realize someone had won a big jackpot tonight.

My job as a dealer at the Treasury Casino means that I get to see all kinds of casino shenanigans each night, from gamblers winning and losing big fortunes to drunken players getting thrown out of the pit for varying reasons. However, through it all, I need to stay focused on the gamblers sitting in front of me and make sure that their experience is a good one.

I've been working at the Treasury for a few years now. There was a time when I hated my job, but these days I've come to appreciate it for what it is—a relatively steady paycheck, for reasonably easy work.

Dealing cards and chatting with gamblers provides a nice contrast from my other job: that of being a private investigator. I had once hoped to quit

"What about her love life?"

Fiona made a facial shrug. "I don't think she was seeing anyone. I mean, she might've been and just not told me, but I doubt it."

"No ex-boyfriends?"

"Not that I know of."

"What about enemies, or anyone who might've wanted to hurt her?"

Fiona sighed. "Ella was a lovely person, and no one would've wanted to hurt her if they knew her. But she was working on a difficult case—the Ronan Hastings rape case."

Ian frowned. "Ronan Hastings? Why does that name sound familiar?"

"Maybe you've heard of him," said Fiona. "He's a twenty-something-year-old who runs a party planning business."

Ian's face lit up and he snapped his fingers. "That's it! I was reading about him the other day in one of those business magazines. He's rich! And he's not running a party planning business—he used to be one of those popular party kids, and now he connects celebrities with rich people who want them at their parties. He knows pretty much all the celebrities and their managers, and he's got lots of contacts. So, let's say some rich guy wants a pop star to sing at his kid's thirteenth birthday party, the rich guy gets in touch with Ronan, who gets in touch with the celebrity and finds out how much it'll cost. And if the deal works out, Ronan takes a cut of it."

"Wow," I said. "That sounds like a great business idea for someone who's well connected."

Ian nodded. "Ronan's rich, and he's kind of famous in some circles."

I turned to Fiona. "Ella was working with this guy?"

"No," said Fiona. "Ronan was being sued by a stripper, Carly Lane, who claimed that he hired her for a bachelor party where she got raped. She's blaming him for being an accessory to the crime, and facilitating it, sort of. Anyway, she was up against Ronan, and he wasn't pleased about it."

I pressed my lips together and nodded. "So, you're saying that this Ronan guy didn't appreciate her presence?"

"One day after court, he came after Ella and told her to drop the case. Said it was ridiculous, and he was innocent and she needed to back down."

My brows knit together. I don't appreciate being threatened or being told to back down from a case, and I didn't like a man who went around threatening other women.

"But that doesn't make sense," said Ian. "Why would Ronan threaten Ella if he wanted the case to be dismissed? Even if Ella stopped working on the case, another lawyer from her firm would work on it. Or the stripper would just hire a different law firm."

Fiona shrugged. "I'm just telling you what Ella told me. She got along with everyone, but this Ronan guy... he clearly didn't like her."

"I have to admit that I agree with Ian," I said slowly. "It doesn't make sense for Ronan to threaten Ella."

"And yet he did," said Fiona. "And the cops barely even talked to him."

"Oh, we'll definitely talk to him," I said quickly. "No doubt about that."

"Besides," said Fiona, "a few days before she died, Ella told me that she'd found out some damaging information. When I asked her what, she said she wanted to look into it a little more before telling anyone."

"And you think it was info about Ronan?"

"What else could it be?" said Fiona. "Ronan must've found out that Ella knew whatever his secret was."

I bit my lip thoughtfully and glanced over at Snowflake, who'd fallen asleep.

Ian said, "It still doesn't make sense, but it sounds like something Ronan might do. The profile I read said that he's a hot-tempered person who likes partying and drinking too much."

"Well, I guess we won't know for sure until we go talk to him," I said steadily. And the fact was, if Ella really had discovered a secret of Ronan's, then Ronan would try his best to keep us from discovering it.

"What about any other enemies?" said Ian. "If Ella was a lawyer, maybe she'd angered other people, too."

"She didn't mention anyone to me," said Fiona. "No one would've gotten angry with Ella personally. I mean, even if you don't like a lawyer, you realize that it's business, not personal."

Ian nodded. "Which is why Ronan's behavior doesn't make sense. Unless Ella discovered his secret, of course."

"There could be something else," I reminded Ian. "Maybe he'd had a little too much to drink, or maybe he was just in a bad mood and wanted to take it out on someone nearby."

Fiona turned to me, looking shocked. "I can't believe you're defending him!"

"I'm not," I said. "It's just that we need to be open

to possibilities. We can't start out an investigation by assuming one person's guilty."

"Of course," said Fiona. "But nobody else had threatened Ella."

"And she wasn't behaving unusually in recent days?"

"No, everything seemed normal."

I chewed my lip thoughtfully and glanced at Ian, wondering if he could think of any other questions, but he just shrugged. Finally, I said, "Is there anything else we should know?"

Fiona shook her head. "I've told you everything I know, and I told the cops the same thing, too."

I nodded thoughtfully. Ronan's behavior was odd, but other than that, it seemed like Ella didn't know anyone who might want to kill her. I could see why the police had written off Ella's death as a mugging gone wrong, and I wondered if I'd have to do the same thing.

ix hours later, I woke up from my nap, took
a quick shower, and headed over to the
living room, where Ian and Snowflake had
set up camp.

After saying goodbye to Fiona, I'd logged Ian in
to my PI database and told him to look up Fiona,
Ella, Ella's friend Felicity, and Ronan Hastings.

Ian was still working on my laptop when I
emerged from my bedroom, ready to face the rest of
the day.

"Find anything interesting?"

Ian shook his head no. "Nothing that
jumps out."

I sighed. It was just as I'd expected, and I was
sure that Ian had been too thorough to overlook
anything. I glanced at my fridge and noticed that

Snowflake was still fast asleep. "Don't tell me she's been sleeping this entire time?"

"So were you," said Ian, sounding a bit defensive. "And she's a cat, she needs to sleep."

I smiled. Snowflake made a pretty cute addition to my kitchen, and I wished I could keep her. "So, what did you find on Ella and Fiona?"

Ian shrugged. "They're both upstanding citizens, three speeding tickets between the two of them, but nothing else. Ella moved to Vegas two years ago and Fiona moved a year ago, just like she told us. I even looked up the law firm where Ella worked—they're a full-service Vegas firm and they've got a great reputation. Employees tend to stay there a long time, so I'm assuming the work environment and pay are pretty good."

"And what about Ella's friend, Felicity?"

"She moved to Vegas four years ago, no priors, not even a speeding ticket."

I nodded glumly. I hadn't expected the database search to reveal much, but I'd still been hoping for a glimmer of something unusual. "And Ronan Hastings?"

"Partygoer and host extraordinaire. He earns a living connecting those who want to party and those who want to perform at rich people's parties, but before that, he was pretty visible on the celebrity party circuit. He even dated a few models and singers and appeared in the tabloids a fair amount—there's interesting gossip about him, but nothing that says he could be a killer."

I sighed. "Even then, I guess we should start off by talking to Ronan. It seems like Ella had no real enemies, and nothing's jumping out in this case— except for Ronan's behavior toward her."

"And the fact that Ella said she'd discovered a secret," Ian reminded me. "If we can uncover Ronan's secret, maybe we could make some quick progress in the case."

I made a face. Ronan sounded like a frivolous, superficial young man, not someone who could be a stone-cold killer. Of course, I might be wrong, and maybe Ronan had had something to do with Ella's death after all.

"We need to shelve all this for now," Ian reminded me, "or we'll be late for lunch at your parents'."

∼

MY PARENTS LIVE up in a northern Vegas suburb, a new one full of large, cheap houses. They moved here after Nanna got married; there's an in-law's suite that offers Nanna and her husband, Wes, privacy and comfort when they're living in Vegas.

Nanna opened the door before Ian and I could knock. Her white hair was curled, her blue eyes as bright as ever, and she peered at me disapprovingly. "No Ryan?"

I stifled my sigh of discontent. "I told you guys already, he's working on an important case and couldn't make the time."

Nanna tut-tutted disapprovingly. "Your mother doesn't think he exists. He didn't come the last few lunches or dinners either."

"He does exist," I said. "We've been dating for a while now."

"A cop," Nanna said as the three of us headed toward the kitchen. "I'd never thought you'd date a cop, what with you being a PI and all. Don't PIs and cops hate each other?"

"Tiffany gets along with most cops," Ian said. "These days."

The kitchen in my parents' new place is a modern white affair, with gleaming white cabinets, white countertops, and modern appliances. A large window looks out onto the desertscaped backyard, and my mother had hung oversized wooden cutlery on one wall.

Mom was adding the finishing touches to the salad, and she gave Ian and me quick hugs. "What's this?" she said, looking at the Tupperware box Ian had brought along.

"Cupcakes," he said. "I made some last night."

My mother beamed at him and gave me a disappointed look. "Now, if only my daughter could learn to bake and cook like that."

"I can bake," I protested. "And I could probably cook if I tried. I just don't have the time."

"You can make time," my mother insisted. "Just like you could make time to be in a real relationship."

I looked at Nanna and sighed.

She shrugged back at me. "Told you. Your mom doesn't believe Ryan exists."

"He does exist," Ian said. "I've met him a couple of times."

"Well," said my mother lightly.

She left it at that, which surprised me. I'd expected a long lecture on how time was running out, nobody wanted to marry a woman over a certain age, let alone a headstrong inept cook, and when was I going to give her grandchildren? But none of that came out of her mouth, which was a relief. I decided to accept her silence on the topic as an unexpected blessing.

"The food'll be ready in a few minutes," my mom said, and the three of us headed over to the den.

Loud exclamations and greetings broke out as soon as Ian and I entered the den. As always, the den was ten degrees cooler than the rest of the house and was slightly dark thanks to the heavy window drapes. Comfy armchairs and sofas were arranged around a TV, and my dad, Karma, Glenn and Wes were sitting and chatting with each other. Although we'd seen everyone in the room within the last few days, it was good to see them again.

"How come you're not watching sports?" I asked my dad as soon as the greetings were over. Dad is a sports fiend, but today there was some kind of dance show playing on the TV.

"It's *Dance Party USA*," said Wes, Nanna's husband. He was a tall, lanky man with a shock of white hair who was usually very quiet. "Your nanna's gotten quite addicted to it."

"I like it, too," said Ian.

"It does look like fun," said Glenn, Wes's older brother. "I've never seen it before, though."

"I have," said Karma, Glenn's girlfriend. She was

a slim gray-haired woman in her fifties who believed in New Age mysticism, Zen teachings, and "clean" eating. "The show has great vibes for something so commercial."

Ian, Nanna and I settled in to watch the show. On the screen, a tall, graceful woman performed an exotic dance routine with her handsome partner.

"Wow," I said when the routine was over. "That was amazing!"

"She's a great dancer," said Nanna. "But the judges will roast her. Just watch."

The camera panned over to three judges who were staring ahead of themselves, looking bored. Two men, one woman. As soon as they realized the camera was on them, they looked all bright-eyed and alert.

The woman judge went first. "That wasn't bad," she said. "But it could do with more... je ne sais quoi."

"That's Francine Pearson," Nanna said. "She's pretty nice."

"It was terrible," said the gray-haired male judge sitting next to her. "We need sparkle."

"That's Carlos," said Ian. "He can be nice or mean, it depends."

The pudgy bald judge went last. "Absolutely

horrendous," he said in a pompous voice. "You've put me to sleep and you'll put anyone who watches you to sleep. Bo-oring."

"Scott Landrum," said Ian. "Big old meanie."

The screen cut to a shot of the woman wiping a tear away, and then the next dancers came onstage.

"Wow," I said. "That was pretty harsh."

"I take back what I said about good vibes," said Karma. "This show's just like all the others."

"It's great!" Nanna insisted. "So much fun."

"It is fun," Ian agreed. "I've always wanted to be a dancer."

"Really?" said Nanna, turning to Ian with intense eyes. "Because I've been thinking, I'd like to enter this show and see how I do. I bet I could give those other dancers a run for their money."

My jaw dropped. This was just the kind of crazy plan Nanna would hatch, and I had no doubt she meant it. How a geriatric woman would compete with lithe semiprofessional dancers was beyond the scope of my imagination, but if anyone could pull this off, it would be Nanna.

Judging from the silence in the room, everyone else was just as surprised by Nanna's idea as I was.

Before I could tell Nanna that maybe she should

consider another hobby, there was a loud knock on the front door.

My mother jumped up, her face shining with delight. "I'll get that."

As soon as she left the room, I looked at Nanna with a grimace. I could just tell that it'd turn out to be another of those horrible men my mother kept trying to set me up with.

Nanna shrugged. "Don't look at me, I don't know what's going on."

"Ryan *does* exist!"

"Maybe," said Nanna noncommittally. "But your mother doesn't believe that."

I was about to go on a rant about cops. The LVMPD has some fine detectives and some not-so-fine ones, and the good guys like Ryan have to pick up the slack caused by the inept. It wasn't Ryan's fault that he'd been called away on an emergency case. I opened my mouth and was just about to get started when my mother walked back into the room. I closed my mouth wordlessly, like a fish.

My mother beamed at the room in general. "Everyone, this is Gavin."

It was then that I noticed the man standing next to her. Just as I'd expected, it was another one of my mother's matchmaking attempts.

Gavin looked youngish, in his mid-twenties or so. Tall, lanky, with straight red hair that fell past his ears. Watery eyes. Skin that looked like the "before" image for an anti-acne face wash.

Introductions were made all around. My mother said, "Gavin is my friend Hugo's son."

I raised an eyebrow at Nanna but said nothing. Until my mother had made it her mission in life to see me settled down with a nice young man, I'd never known that she had so many friends with eligible sons.

Gavin said he worked as a stagehand at a local media production company. "It's not that much money," he said, "but it's fun working on the Vegas episodes of popular TV shows."

"That sounds exciting!" Nanna said. "I could use some more excitement in my life."

I groaned.

My mother said, "You're always chasing excitement. When are you going to settle down?"

"Never, if I can help it. I keep telling Tiff I can help out on her cases, but she hardly ever lets me."

"No cases," my mother and I said simultaneously. For once, we were in agreement. The last time Nanna had insisted on helping out on a case, she'd managed to get a murderer quite annoyed at us.

"Well," said Nanna, "if you don't want me helping out on murder cases, what's a girl to do?"

"Working on cases isn't all that exciting," said Ian. "I could use some more excitement in my life, too. Especially now that I'm avoiding women."

Ian has a disastrous track record with women—mostly thanks to his own cluelessness, and the fact that all the women he attracts seem to be gold diggers who are well aware of his trust fund.

"We could enter *Dance Party USA* together!" Nanna said gleefully. She turned to look at Gavin. "Isn't *Dance Party USA* going to hold auditions in Vegas soon?"

Gavin looked at her apologetically. "I don't really know, I'm not working on that show."

"They are," said Karma. "I just heard them talking about it when Gavin walked in."

"There you go!" said Nanna. "It's a sign. Ian and I have to enter."

"I don't think signs work like that," said Karma. "They're much more subtle. I'm not getting a good vibe about you two entering the show."

I frowned. While I find Karma a little too New Age-y, her "vibes" have often turned out to be true.

"Nonsense!" said Nanna. "I need some excitement in my life, and this seems perfect."

"I wouldn't mind entering," said Ian. "I'm good at reality TV shows and auditions and stuff. Tiffany and I entered a singing show once, and we got through the audition."

"You froze when you got onstage," I reminded Ian.

"So did you," he countered.

"Well... I guess you're right," I admitted. "We both froze. We only got through because of our investigation with one of the judges."

"Still," said Ian, "the point is, I've got experience. And I'd like to audition again! It'll be fun."

"Lunch is getting cold," my mother said suddenly. She frowned, glancing at Gavin, who was sitting quietly in one corner, and then gave me a pointed look. Clearly, the two of us should be getting to know each other already. "Let's go sit down."

We headed to the dining room, where the large table was already laden with food—my mother must've set it while we'd all been chatting about *Dance Party USA*.

Unsurprisingly, Gavin and I wound up sitting next to each other. Nanna sat on my other side, and Ian sat opposite her.

We helped ourselves to the food, and I dug in as soon as politely possible. My mother had outdone herself—the roast lamb was tender and succulent, the mashed potatoes were creamy and smooth, and even the roast veggies were delicious.

As I concentrated on my food, Nanna leaned across me and said to Gavin, "You must have contacts in all the Vegas production companies. I'm sure you'll know when they start auditioning."

"I can ask around," said Gavin politely. "Maybe I can find something out for you. Although usually, they ask you to mail in a tape first."

Ian nodded sagely. "Exactly. We'll have to create an audition tape."

I groaned. "You two aren't seriously considering this, are you?"

"What're you talking about?" said Nanna. "It's a great idea!"

I looked at Wes, who was sitting opposite me, but he just smiled and shrugged. "I'm happy if Gwenda's happy. If she wants to enter a dance competition with Ian, she should. You only live once."

My dad and Glenn were deep in conversation about some football team, and my mother was glaring at Nanna for hogging Gavin's conversation time. Only Karma seemed slightly concerned. So I said to her, "What's this bad vibe of yours about?"

She shook her head. "It's not clear. But there's

something bad associated with this dance show. I think it leads to something bad, but I can't see for sure."

Nanna turned to Gavin again. "Ian and I'll mail in a tape. Could you ask around and see what they're looking for? I've already got a pretty good idea, since I watch the show all the time, but I wouldn't mind some insider information."

My mother said sharply, "I'm sure Gavin didn't come to lunch to talk about work."

"I don't mind," Gavin said politely. "I like my work, and it seems like Nanna and Ian really want to enter the show."

I looked at him suspiciously. He seemed like a perfectly nice guy on the surface, but the men my mother invites home for meals have always turned out to be strange, slimy specimens of human nature.

"Why don't I change spots with Nanna?" I suggested. "Then you two can chat about the show."

"Don't be rude," said my mother sharply. She wasn't about to let her hopes for me and Gavin fade away into oblivion, thanks to Nanna's penchant for dance reality shows. "I'm sure you and Gavin have a lot to talk about, too."

I sighed. I didn't mean to be rude, but it was

tiring to be set up with all these men, especially when I had a boyfriend.

"I'm looking forward to getting to know you better," said Gavin with a smile.

Automatically, I said, "I have a boyfriend."

My mother said, "Whom we've never met. I mean, if he really was your boyfriend, wouldn't he come over for a meal?"

"He's a cop—he's working on an urgent case!"

"Sounds like he's really busy," said Gavin.

"He is." I looked at him and smiled. He wasn't all that bad.

"You know," said Gavin, "I'm sure you're like Nanna and Ian—you probably wouldn't mind some excitement in your life, would you?"

I frowned, trying to decipher what he meant, when there it was. His hot, clammy hand grabbing my upper thigh under the dining table.

Instinctively, I grabbed his forefinger and pulled it backward.

I stopped myself before I could do any real damage. No point breaking a man's finger just because he was a bad judge of character.

"No," I said, smiling sweetly at him, "I don't like excitement."

Gavin's face had gone all clenched up, his eyes narrowed in pain.

"Gavin," my mother said, "are you all right?"

I let go of his finger.

Immediately, the hand disappeared from my thigh, and Gavin took a deep breath in, relaxing his muscles. "No. I mean, yes. I'm all right. I'm fine."

He didn't look at me for the next five minutes and focused on his food. Karma started talking to my mother about some mutual friend of theirs, and Nanna and Ian chatted some more about how to enter a dance competition.

"I'm a really good dancer," Ian was saying. "I can do all kinds of moves."

"I'm pretty good too," said Nanna. "I was a real hit at the senior center dances. Everyone wanted to dance with me. Too bad for them I met Wes."

Wes and Nanna shared a smile, and I found myself smiling at them and feeling all mushy inside.

A voice drifted over from next to me.

"So, Tiffany, do you like dancing too?"

I looked at Gavin in surprise. He was smiling, and he looked as though he'd forgotten all about the finger incident.

"No," I said. "I don't."

"That's too bad. I like dancing. I could've taken you dancing if you wanted."

"No, thanks."

My mother drifted out of her conversation with Karma long enough to overhear me turning down Gavin's invite. "That's not true," she said. "Tiffany loves dancing. I'm sure she'd love to go dancing with you."

Gavin smiled and put his hand on my knee.

I sighed, rolled my eyes, and pushed his hand away.

"You don't seem to get it," I said to him politely. "I'm really not interested."

Nanna elbowed me from the other side. "Don't be rude, Tiffany. Gavin's going to help us get onto *Dance Party USA*."

I looked at her in exasperation. Of course, she had no idea that Gavin liked to grab body parts under the table, but I couldn't help rolling my eyes.

"We should all go to the *Dance Party USA* audition together," said Ian enthusiastically. I shot daggers at him with my eyes, but he ignored me. "If we get in, that is."

"I'm sure you'll get in," said Gavin. "It'll be fun to go together."

He looked at me and grinned, and I wondered

what it'd take for this man to get the message. On the other hand, I was sure that the chances of Nanna and Ian getting through to even the first audition round were slim to none.

"That sounds good," Nanna was saying. "Now we just have to practice a little and make that audition tape."

"I can help out," Gavin said. "I'm happy to help out."

He looked at me, smiled and put his hand back on my knee.

I pushed it off in an instant and said, "I know Krav Maga. And my boyfriend's a cop."

But he continued smiling at me hopefully, refusing to take the hint.

5

Nanna and Ian kept going on about their dance audition, and after lunch we lingered over dessert and coffee. At some point, I managed to switch seats with Nanna without my mother complaining too much—Gavin said something about meeting me for a meal someday, so that seemed to please her.

When we got into the car, I turned to Ian and said, "I wish you wouldn't be so nice to Gavin! He's pretty awful."

I filled Ian in on Gavin's grabbiness as we drove toward the station, but he just shrugged.

"He's harmless," Ian said. "And I really do want to enter this dance thing. I need some excitement in my life. Besides, you probably won't ever see Gavin again."

I had to agree with that last statement, so I pushed the man out of my mind and concentrated on what questions we needed to ask about Ella's death.

The LVMPD offices are housed in a building west of the Strip. The exterior is boring red brick, and the interior is boring white and gray. Ian and I've been here so often that most of the detectives know us, and since we tend not to meddle with open cases too often, they don't mind us too much.

We headed straight to the bullpen in search of Detective Elwood. Ian had called the precinct while I'd been asleep. He'd found out that Elwood had been the detective in charge of the case and managed to get an appointment for the two of us.

Detective Elwood is a chubby, balding man with a perpetual scowl. We've run into him on many cases before, and while we didn't get off on the right foot, I'd like to think that he's got a grudging respect for us by now. That, plus we've been giving him cupcakes whenever we go to talk to him.

He was sitting at his desk, going through some paperwork, when Ian and I arrived. When he saw us, the first words out of his mouth were, "Did you bring any cupcakes?"

"Sorry," I said. "Ian baked some more of those

delicious hazelnut cupcakes, but we ate them all! They were even more delicious than those last ones we gave you."

Elwood's scowl deepened and his face darkened. He glanced at the mug of stale coffee sitting on his desk and said, "Those hazelnut cupcakes go really well with coffee."

"Yes, they do," said Ian brightly.

Elwood stared at his coffee mug glumly. He'd become addicted to Ian's cupcakes, and he knew it. "I could just go to a bakery and buy a cupcake from them," he muttered, almost to himself.

"You could," I said. "But it probably wouldn't be as good."

Elwood sighed and looked at us. The question hung in the air, and before he could ask it, Ian said, "It's okay, we'll bring you some cupcakes next time we come over."

Elwood's lips began to twist upwards in a rare smile, and he stopped himself just in time and looked at us skeptically instead. "You're not going to forget, are you? Or eat them all up again?"

"We're not," said Ian, "I promise."

"I'm not making any promises," I said. "Everyone knows how much I love cupcakes!"

Elwood looked at me glumly, and I felt sorry for him.

"It's okay," I reassured him, "I was just kidding."

He scowled. "You've got a terrible sense of humor."

"I keep telling her that," said Ian. "But I guess she makes up for it by being a good investigator."

"Speaking of which," I said, "we're here to talk about the Ella Miller case."

Elwood sighed. "Of course you are."

"You're not going to give us a hard time about the info, are you?"

"Like you gave me a hard time about the cupcakes?" Elwood shook his head. "Wait here, I'll go get the files."

I resisted the urge to peek at Elwood's paperwork while we waited for him.

A few minutes later, he was back, and he flipped through the file before handing it over to us.

"Ella Miller was killed near Balzar Avenue," he said. "I don't need to tell you two what that part of town's like. Who in their right mind goes there all alone after nine o'clock at night? Anyway, we found the body at two a.m., and forensics put time of death at between ten and eleven at night. Shot through the stomach, three times. No witnesses. No purse or jewelry found on the body, indicating it was a mugging. We talked to the victim's associates, but nobody had any motive to hurt her. Nothing to indicate that this was anything premeditated."

I flipped through the file quickly and then handed it over to Ian. The file said pretty much everything that Elwood had told me, and Ella's list of "associates" included the people that Fiona had told me about, plus her coworkers.

I said, "It says here that the autopsy found traces of calamari salad in her stomach."

"So?" said Elwood. "Not like calamari salad is rare."

"No. But it's not the kind of thing you'd cook at home."

Elwood shrugged. "Maybe she ate out, then went for a walk near Balzar. Or maybe she ordered in."

"In which case, she'd have had leftovers in her fridge, but the file doesn't mention any. Plus, how'd she get to that neighborhood anyway? It's not like she could've walked. And the report says you talked to the cab companies, but she hadn't taken a cab."

Elwood rolled his eyes. "So you got me. But we talked to the neighbors, and nobody'd given her a ride or seen her getting picked up."

"Doesn't mean she wasn't picked up."

"Yeah," Elwood admitted. "That's the most likely explanation. Someone picked her up around dinner-time and all the neighbors were too busy with their own lives to notice."

"So who picked her up? Nobody you interviewed said they'd given her a lift that night."

"Maybe she met someone online," Elwood suggested. "You know, using one of those phone apps. And the man picked her up and took her to dinner, where she had a calamari salad."

"And then he dropped her off near Balzar Avenue?"

"Maybe they had a fight."

I thought about Handsy Gavin. Maybe Ella's date had gone bad and she'd left the car in a rush... but wait, why was I buying into Elwood's theory?

Ian finished going through the file and said, "You talked to Ronan Hastings."

"We did. And he had an alibi for that night—he was at a party with a bunch of his friends."

"Did you ask him about the fight he'd had earlier with Ella?"

Elwood rolled his eyes. "Look, you're a cop in Vegas, you don't mess with rich people, okay? Because doing that just results in a call from the mayor, and then the chief has to tell you to lay off."

Ian said, "So you didn't really ask him about his fight with Ella?"

"Sure we did," said Elwood. "He told us he'd been in a bad mood that day and took it out on the lawyer. Nothing personal."

I pressed my lips together, not really believing that story. "And you followed up on his alibi?"

"Of course," said Elwood. "Went through the list of ten friends he'd given us and called three of them at random. They all said that Ronan had been with them all night."

I frowned. "Hmm."

"Ronan's got nothing to do with Ella's death," said Elwood. "I know he's telling the truth, I can just tell."

I trusted Elwood's instincts much less than I trusted Karma's.

Ian and I rifled through the file a little more and tried to chat with Elwood, who remained adamant that Ella's death must've been a random act of violence. But the more I looked at the report, the more I felt like something was missing.

Ian and I mused about it on the short drive home.

"If someone's murdered," said Ian, "usually the motive's love or money."

"And Ella had no wealth worth killing for."

"So, the motive must've been love."

"But according to her sister, she wasn't seeing anyone."

"Maybe it was a secret. Maybe she was seeing someone who needed privacy. Maybe she was seeing Ronan!"

"I don't think it'll be that simple," I said. "But I don't think Ronan's as innocent as Elwood says he is. We'd better go talk to him and see if he's hiding something."

Ronan didn't sound all that pleased when I called and introduced myself, but he wasn't explicitly rude either.

"I can meet you in a few hours," he said. "But I can't talk long."

I assured him that our conversation wouldn't take too long, and then Ian and I stopped back at my apartment. I called in sick at the casino; it's not something I like to do, but I wanted to talk to Ronan as soon as possible. Thankfully, nobody at the Treasury gives me grief for my occasional sick days, and I knew that my shift would be covered by someone else.

Ian brought Snowflake over to hang out with us, but she chose to jump back on top of the fridge and watch us with curious blue eyes.

Ian said to me, "Maybe we can make some of those lemon-buttercream cupcakes we talked about before we need to go meet Ronan."

I couldn't help getting swept up in Ian's enthusiasm for making the cupcakes, but I felt a twinge of guilt. Every now and then, I'd help Ian with his baking, which meant that I'd soon have the ability to make cupcakes whenever I felt like it. But I'd never learned to do actual *cooking*; at this rate, my diet would soon consist mostly of cupcakes.

"Maybe we should learn to make some healthy food," I said thoughtfully. "You know, stir-fried veggies and stuff."

Ian looked mystified. "Why?"

"I'm not sure," I admitted. "It seems like the adult thing to do."

"Well, you're always bringing leftovers from your parents', and we order takeout a lot, and there's always microwave meals. You can make salads and sandwiches."

"Lots of cafes serve only salads and sandwiches," I said, feeling a little better about the whole thing. "But what if... my mother keeps saying that I need to learn to cook if I want to get married. Maybe she's getting to me."

Ian whipped up some eggs in a large mixing

bowl and poured in some sugar. "I never thought you'd be eager to get married."

I chewed my lip thoughtfully and wondered about my relationship with Ryan. "I like Ryan a lot," I said as Ian added some lemon extract and melted butter to his mixture. "But I'm not sure where we're going. I mean, we've never talked about long-term stuff, and he hasn't even met my parents yet."

"Mostly because you kept the relationship a secret from them," Ian reminded me.

"I know," I admitted. And then there was Stone. For a long time, I'd felt something between us, something that had exploded when finally, one day, we'd kissed. However, the next day, men in dark suits had shown up looking for him, and Stone had had to go underground. I've finally learned the truth about Stone's past, and I'm waiting for things to clear up—but even if they do, Stone's always warned me that he's not a relationship person. And now that I know about his past, I don't blame him.

"Ryan seems like a great guy," Ian said. "Really nice. And he seems to want to get more serious with you."

"That's true," I admitted. "I'm just not sure myself." Because of Stone, I thought to myself. Who I hadn't even seen in ages.

Ian had added some more ingredients to his mixture while we'd talked, and now it had taken on the thick, yummy-looking consistency of cupcake batter.

"What about you?" I said as Ian went to work on the frosting. "Are you really taking a break from women?"

"Maybe," he said. "I just don't know how to make progress. Vegas isn't a great place to look for people who want real relationships."

I sighed. "Yeah. It's easier to stick to loving cupcakes and kittens."

RONAN WAS STAYING in the Presidential Suite at the Mauritian Casino, an upscale place on the north end of the Strip. We had to take a special elevator up that stopped in front of the entrance to his suite, and when we knocked, Ronan opened the door himself.

He turned out to be a short, muscular man with jet-black hair, piercing blue eyes and a serious expression. "Ian and Tiffany?" he said.

"That's us," Ian said. "And you're Ronan Hastings. I read about you in a magazine the other day."

That got a smile out of him. "Don't believe everything you read," he said, leading us inside.

The living room of the suite was done in a white and aqua theme: white fabric sofas with aqua cushions, and a large painting of the ocean on one wall. The wall opposite us was floor-to-ceiling glass, a massive window looking out onto the Strip.

As we settled in, Ronan said, "I've already talked to the cops about Ella Miller's death. I don't know what else I can say."

"We've been hired by Ella's sister," I said politely. "We've already looked at the police files, but I like to talk to everyone myself."

Ronan shrugged. "Sure."

"You knew Ella because of the case she was working on."

"Yep."

"Can you tell us some more about the case?"

Ronan pressed his lips together and looked out the window. It was obvious that his lawyer must've told him not to say too much, and he was wondering why he'd ever agreed to meet us.

"It's a stupid case," he said finally. "Some woman suing me because I arranged the party. I had nothing to do with the crime. It was a large suite, and I was in the living area drinking with the others."

I watched him carefully. His expression was guarded and his tone defensive. I wondered if the plaintiff really had a case against him, and how much this was bothering him.

"You must get sued all the time," Ian said sympathetically. "Since you're pretty popular and all that."

Ronan looked at him. "My lawyers handle it. Scammers chasing a quick buck is all it is—we can usually shut them down with an official letter or two."

I said, "But that's not what's happening with the case Ella was working on."

Ronan turned to us, annoyance flashing in his eyes. "I can't talk about that case."

"Of course, your lawyers must've told you not to."

He nodded wordlessly, his expression blank.

I said, "And what about Ella? Why did you threaten her?"

Ronan sighed. "I didn't threaten her, I just told her to back off."

"Sounds like the same thing to me," said Ian. "But I'm not very good at threatening people."

Ronan rolled his eyes. "Look, I was having a bad day, okay? First, I had a pop star pull out of a party at the last minute, and the hosts decided that meant they wouldn't pay me my cut. Even though I'd done my job. You know how it is with celebrities. You gotta charge upfront 'cause everyone's always changing their minds about stuff. And then, my PA said she'd quit, and she was a damn good PA too. And then, this court thing. Ella kept coming after me, saying stuff, and I lost my cool. So afterward, I went and gave her a piece of my mind before my lawyer could stop me. I regret it now, of course. How was I supposed to know the woman was going to go get herself killed?"

I tried not to narrow my eyes. "So, you regret going after Ella because now she's dead? And you've got to deal with these questions?"

"That's not what I meant," Ronan snapped irritably. "I mean, yes, it's an annoyance dealing with people like you, but I could've just not met you, right?"

That thought had occurred to me as well. If Ronan had something to hide, he wouldn't meet up with PIs, who, unlike cops, couldn't force him to talk. "Then what *did* you mean?"

He ran a hand through his hair. "You know how it is. One day you're alive and the next day you're not. I wouldn't have gone after her so hard if I'd known she'd up and die."

I looked at him skeptically. "Hmm."

"I've got a bad temper, that's all. I guess I say stuff when I shouldn't."

I nodded. He did seem contrite about haranguing a woman who'd died shortly afterward; perhaps he'd felt guilty enough about it that he'd agreed to talk to us. "What did she say that made you so angry?"

Ronan's brows knit together. "Everything. Every word out of her mouth—going after me. Made it out like I'm some kind of supervillain."

I said, "You did facilitate a party where a girl was raped."

Ronan shook his head emphatically. "I'm not that guy. I had no idea what was happening. Nothing like this ever happened before. And I help host lots of parties."

"Maybe it has, and no one's spoken out before."

Ronan looked at me in silence, and I saw a mix of emotions in his eyes. I tried to decipher what they were—fear, guilt, anger, disappointment?

He shook his head again. "Anyway, I got mad at Ella that day, is all. I didn't really know her otherwise."

Ian said, "Ella knew a secret about you."

Ronan blinked and looked at him in surprise. "What?"

"Something about you that no one knew."

A corner of his mouth went up quizzically. "I didn't even know I had any secrets left."

Ian and I exchanged a glance. He seemed to believe it.

"Something about the case, then," I said. "Something that no one else knew."

Ronan shrugged. "I don't deal with the case, my lawyer does."

I frowned. "Did you and Ella talk about anything in particular?"

"No, I just told her to back off, and that I didn't like her blaming me for what happened. I had nothing to do with it, and she and her client knew that."

"And you didn't talk about anything else?"

He shook his head. "I usually don't talk to people I don't know very well. I have to craft my image in the media super carefully, and I'm not going to mess that up by blabbing to randoms."

Ian said, "Did you ever talk to her before that day?"

"Hell, no," said Ronan. "My lawyer would've killed me if I did."

"And," I said, feeling stupid even as I started

asking the question, "you weren't seeing her in secret or something?"

Ronan let out a bark of laughter. "No way. I stick to models and wannabe actresses and singers. They're much more fun than stuck-up lawyers. Besides, they look better in my Insta photos."

I nodded thoughtfully. So far, I believed Ronan's words, which was ironic—I'd come into the interview expecting to hate him or uncover some kind of dark secret. Either he was a very good actor, or he was telling us the truth.

"And what about the night Ella died?" I said. "Where were you?"

Ronan looked at me with eyes that were polite but steely. "I've already told the cops, I was at a party at the Deadly Disco. Twenty of my friends saw me there, and I'm sure they've called up people to ask."

I nodded, unable to think of anything else to ask.

"You seem to have pretty good luck with women," said Ian. "And you're pretty rich. Whenever I meet someone, they find out I've got a trust fund and then things don't work out. Tiffany thinks I only attract gold diggers."

Ronan turned to him sympathetically. "That's just how it is, man. Some women just want your money."

"Do women you meet just want your money?"

Ronan shrugged. "I don't keep them long enough to find out. We have some fun, then I cut them loose."

"Hmm," said Ian, furrowing his brow. "I think I'd like to keep someone around. Being in a real relationship would be fun."

Ronan's features softened for a minute. "Yeah, that would be nice. But I've given up on it. Even when I meet someone I want to keep around, they'll probably want my money."

Ian smiled encouragingly. "Maybe not. Maybe you'll meet someone who cares about more than money."

Ronan shook his head, not seeming convinced. "Here in Vegas? Doubtful. Possible, but doubtful."

Ronan and Ian got into a conversation about how Ronan had started his company, and I watched thoughtfully. Ronan was different from what I'd expected; he was genuine, and he actually seemed like a reasonably nice person.

I couldn't think of anything else to ask him, and when Ronan and Ian were done chatting, we said our goodbyes.

"Call me if you think of anything else," I said to

Ronan, handing him my card just before I stepped into the elevator. "Anything at all."

Ronan smiled politely. "Sure. But I don't think I'll think of anything."

As the elevator doors closed, I thought I saw a change in Ronan's expression: I was pretty sure that was a flicker of relief in his eyes. But before I could say something, the elevator headed downwards, taking us away from him and his private suite.

7

As Ian and I drove over to Deadly Disco, I said, "Did you think Ronan was lying?"

Ian shrugged. "He seemed kind of nice."

"Yes, but that doesn't mean he's not lying about something."

"Okay. But what could he be lying about?"

"Anything! That's the thing about people who are good actors—you don't know when they're acting."

Ian frowned. "What makes you think he's lying?"

I told Ian about the glimmer of relief I thought I'd seen in Ronan's eyes as we were leaving.

"That doesn't mean he was lying to us," Ian said optimistically. "Maybe he was just annoyed by all my questions about work. Or maybe he doesn't like talking to people."

"He's a party organizer! Of course he likes talking to people."

"Okay, maybe it's just PIs that he doesn't like talking to."

"Hmm." I wasn't convinced, but maybe Ian had a point. Maybe Ronan's relief had been about something else.

When we arrived at Deadly Disco, it was almost seven in the evening, far too early for the club to open its doors.

The bouncer nodded at Ian and me, recognizing us from a previous investigation, and we headed inside.

The large dance floor was empty, dark and lit with overhead strobe lights. The place was eerily quiet, and at the far end, over by the bar, a man was getting things set up. Ian and I headed straight for the door on one side, marked "Staff Only," and walked through the hallway on the other side.

There were doors leading to staff offices on either side of the hallway, and I knew that one of the doors led to an employee break room and another to an employee bathroom. I knocked on the door to the club owner's office, but there was no response.

Instead, a voice from across the hallway said, "He's not in, but maybe I can help you guys."

The voice belonged to Kara, the owner's assistant, and Ian and I went over to her room and exchanged hellos. Kara was a skinny brunette in her mid-thirties with dark eyes and an expression that belied her efficiency. Her room was tiny, crammed with a small desk and a couple of chairs. A poster of New York hung on one wall. The desk held a computer and a stack of papers, and the room smelled of pine air freshener.

"It's been a while since I've seen you two," Kara said. "What've you been up to?"

"Not much," I said. "Just doing the usual investigating stuff."

"It's been pretty boring, really," said Ian. "I'm thinking of entering a dance competition for fun."

"I didn't know you danced," said Kara. "Which competition?"

"*Dance Party USA!*"

Kara's face lit up. "I watch that show! It's so much fun—but they're professional dancers, mostly."

"I'm really good," Ian insisted.

Kara and I exchanged a glance. Neither of us believed him.

"Well, good luck," she said. "Let me know if you get in."

"I will," said Ian. "I'm going to enter with Tiffany's nanna. It'll be fun."

Ian and Kara talked some more about reality shows and how much fun they were to watch, and then she turned to me. "I'm assuming you're here on an investigation?"

"Yes, we're checking the alibi of a guy who was here two weeks ago. Ronan Hastings."

Kara nodded. "I remember that night. He brought a bunch of models along, and business was good all week. I'll go fish out the surveillance camera files. You can watch them on my computer."

Ian and I thanked her, and once she'd set everything up, we settled in to watch.

I said, "Ella's time of death was estimated at around ten or eleven, so we just need to watch around that time."

I started with the first camera, but Ronan didn't appear on screen during that time. So I moved on to the files for the second camera—but still no Ronan. The same thing happened with all the videos we watched; Ronan was nowhere to be seen.

We watched again, starting from earlier in the

day, but the last time Ronan was recorded on camera was at eight thirty, when he was seen heading toward the door and stepping out.

Things were not looking good.

"Maybe he left, and then re-entered through the private rear entrance," said Ian. "And then maybe he somehow stayed in the cameras' blind spots the rest of the night."

I looked at Kara, who was sitting opposite us and working through a stack of mail. "Is it possible to stay in blind spots for a while?"

Kara shook her head. "There are a few blind spots, but no one could stay in them for more than a minute or two, at most."

I pressed my lips together and exhaled slowly through my nose.

Ian was frowning. "I didn't see this coming," he said.

"Me neither," I admitted. "Elwood said Ronan's friends vouched for his presence at the club."

"They could be lying."

"I'm sure they are. But we may as well call them all and see if anyone wants to say something different about Ronan's whereabouts that night."

IAN and I headed back home. We found Snowflake fast asleep on Ian's bed and headed to my apartment without her, where we spent a depressingly long time calling through the list of Ronan's friends.

I called ten people, and Ian called ten. All of them answered on the first call; they were clearly people who were tied to their phones.

"Sure," said everyone I talked to. "I was with Ronan that night. We were busy partying at the Deadly Disco. He was there all night, until I left after midnight. No, I didn't talk to him after eight thirty, but he was hanging out with the other guys. Yes, I'm sure of it. No, I wasn't too drunk to remember; no, Ronan didn't tell me to say all this."

By the time I was done, I was ready to rip my hair out in chunks.

I got through my list before Ian and made myself a mug of decaf while I waited. When he was finished, Ian turned to me and said, "Ronan sure has good friends."

"I think he's paying them." I was fuming, disappointed at how easily people lied. "I can't believe this."

Ian shrugged. "I guess that's just how it is."

"And Elwood never picked up on it."

"Maybe there was something wrong with the surveillance cameras..."

"I highly doubt that. Now I'm convinced that Ronan's hiding something—why else would he bother to make up an alibi?"

Ian chewed a fingernail thoughtfully. "You don't think Ronan actually killed Ella, do you? He seemed to mean it when he was talking about how he wished he hadn't yelled at Ella. How can you regret yelling at someone if you killed them?"

I shook my head. "I don't know what's going on, but Ronan's definitely hiding something."

"Are we heading back to see Ronan again?"

I shook my head. "He'll probably be out dealing with clients, this time of night." I glanced at the clock—Ian and I had been so busy calling up Ronan's friends that we'd skipped dinner. "And it's not like we can just barge into his suite."

I called Ronan, and when he learned it was me, his voice grew wary.

"How can I help you?" he said politely.

"There's something we seem to have over-looked," I said. "How soon can we come talk to you again?"

"I'm at dinner with a client, but I've got five

minutes. Why don't you ask me now? I'm busy all day tomorrow and most of the next."

"I'm not much of a phone person." This was partly true; in my experience, people have an easier time avoiding the truth over the phone. Face-to-face, you can try to read a person's expressions and body language—even if they're a good actor. "How soon can we meet you?"

"Day after tomorrow's the earliest. No, the day after that. You sure we can't do this over the phone?"

I screwed up my face thoughtfully, not wanting to wait so long to talk to Ronan. I said, "We had a look at the Deadly Disco surveillance tapes. You disappeared early in the night."

I'd expected Ronan to deny it, but he just said, "I see."

There was a long pause, both of us waiting for the other to talk first. I haven't been a private investigator for long, but I knew that silence was an important part of the game.

Finally, Ronan said, "You've looked at *all* the tapes?"

"We have."

I expected Ronan to say something about staying in the camera blind spots for the rest of the night, or maybe blaming malfunctioning surveillance equipment. Thankfully, he didn't try to insult my intelligence. Instead, he said, "The cops never asked me about it, so I never told them."

"I understand."

"A guy like me—you know I've got a reputation to protect, right? So I let them believe I was at the club all night."

"But you weren't."

"No."

"Where were you?"

Ronan sighed and said in a hushed voice, "I can't tell you right now. There are too many people around me."

"Oh-kay..."

"But trust me, I've got proof of where I was that night. And it was nowhere near Ella."

"Uh-huh."

"Look, I'll tell you when I meet you next. In three days' time, right?"

I pressed my lips together. I couldn't force Ronan to tell me what was going on, and what choice did I have about when to meet him? "Sure," I said.

We decided on a time, and then Ronan hung up, sounding relieved to be done chatting with me.

I turned to Ian, annoyed that I'd have to wait three days before talking to Ronan. I filled him in on the conversation and said, "Ronan's hiding something."

Ian nodded, looking slightly disheartened. "I'd thought he was nice."

"So did I. I guess he's not."

"But maybe he's got a good alibi. He said he could prove where he was."

"That's an odd thing to bluff about," I admitted. "Maybe Ronan wasn't the one who shot Ella, but why would he lie about his whereabouts in the first place? Something about him is off. He's definitely got a secret."

Just then, my phone rang. It wasn't a number I recognized, and when I answered it, a voice on the other end said, "This is Gavin."

I couldn't hide my disappointment. "Oh. My mother must've given you my number."

"Yeah—she said you'd want to talk about *Dance Party USA*. I talked to one of the guys working on the show and—"

"You'll want to talk to Ian about that," I said abruptly, cutting Gavin off and handing the phone over to Ian. I was relieved to have gotten out of a conversation with Grabby Gavin, and I hoped he wouldn't call me again.

Ian and Gavin chatted for a few minutes and then Ian hung up and turned to me, beaming. "This is awesome! The deadline for video auditions was a week ago, but Gavin managed to pull some strings and now Nanna and I can enter!"

I looked at him skeptically. "What do you need to do?"

"We have to make a video tomorrow. It'll be Nanna and me dancing, showing off what we can do. I can't wait."

"But Karma said it wasn't a good idea."

"Since when do you pay attention to Karma's 'vibes'?"

"Since she made those predictions that came true. Her intuition's not too bad."

Ian flipped one hand dismissively. "Ah, phooey. She got lucky once or twice. Besides, maybe the bad thing she's worried about is that Nanna and I'll be sad if the judges are mean. But we'll be okay, we're tough."

I looked at Ian warily. Perhaps he had a point. Perhaps Karma was wrong about this. Maybe it'd be good for Nanna to enter the competition and have some fun.

"Okay," I said, trying to be supportive. "Maybe you and Nanna'll make a good dancing couple."

Even as I said the words, I had to bite back a chuckle. A man with two left feet and a seventy-five-year-old with arthritis entering a dance reality show —what could go wrong?

8

I caught some extra z's since I'd already canceled my shift at the Treasury, and the next morning, I fought off the urge to have lemon-buttercream cupcakes for breakfast. Instead, Ian and I headed over to Neil's Diner, a local hangout just off-Strip, for a slightly healthier breakfast. Ian had pancakes with berries and whipped cream ("Berries have antioxidants! This really *is* a healthy breakfast!") and I had bacon, eggs and hash browns.

I couldn't stop thinking about Ronan's blatant deceit regarding his alibi, but it was time to head to Ella's law firm and talk to people there.

The law firm was housed in a massive glass-walled building just west of Freemont Street. The exterior was impressive, with palm trees interspersed with hedges flanking the front entrance, and the lobby inside was cool and pristine, with white marble and a trio of elevators against the far wall.

Elman and Associates occupied the tenth and eleventh floors, and we headed straight to the eleventh floor, where the senior partners' offices were. The office smelled of money, with its hushed vibe, crisp air freshener and muted sense of stress and frantic work. The floors were a dark wood, the walls decorated with expensive-looking art, and the employees we passed by wore well-fitting dark suits.

Our first appointment was with Sam Gooding, and when we approached the receptionist, a sleek brunette wearing thick-rimmed glasses, she pointed us in the direction of his office.

Ian and I walked past a large open-space area teeming with young suited people busily typing away and rifling through files, over to the other end of the floor. There were glass-walled offices on this side, each with a nameplate on its door. The offices all had blinds that could be drawn for privacy, but all the blinds were open. I guessed the head honchos prided themselves on "values" like openness and transparency; or perhaps they just liked to show off their nice offices.

I peered inside as I knocked on the door to Sam's

office. It seemed like one of the bigger rooms, furnished to impart a sense of luxury: Persian carpet on the floor; big wooden desk; comfy upholstered seats for the clients.

Sam looked up at the knock, smiled, and waved us in. He seemed to be in his late fifties and was handsome in a way that implied a lot of grooming. Thick eyebrows, clear blue eyes, skin that hinted at subtle Botox, and a full head of dark blond hair.

"You must be Tiffany and Ian," he said. "It's nice to meet you."

I murmured something about how kind he was to make time for us, and Sam waved away my half-apology.

"I'm happy to try to help," he said. "Ella was very popular here, and we're sorry to lose her."

He spoke as though Ella had decided to quit to take a tour of Europe, and I nodded politely. "Thank you. What can you tell us about her?"

"She was wonderful," he said, smiling at us. "Very efficient, very intelligent. Hard worker, charming with the clients, great personality. We had high hopes for her at the office. She could've been partner one day." His smile faded as he thought back to the kind of person Ella had been. "A lot of young people are ambitious," he said thoughtfully, "but

Ella was diligent. Thorough with her work. Conscientious."

"Other associates must've been jealous of her," I suggested, "if she was that good."

Sam shrugged. "We encourage a healthy sense of competition among the younger employees. It doesn't hurt. But if you're implying that someone..." He shook his head. "Employees are promoted based on merit, or recommendations from the senior employees they've worked with. Nobody here would hurt Ella."

"I'm sure you're right," I said, "but I still have to ask. Did you know if anyone here disliked Ella?"

Sam shook his head. His eyes were piercing and thoughtful, and I wondered if his high regard for Ella included an attraction that went beyond the professional. He wore a wedding ring, but my experience of rich old men has been that a wedding ring sometimes doesn't mean all that much. He said, "I don't get involved in employee politics. And the senior staff all liked her."

Ian said, "You have a really cool office. I like how one wall is all windows. Just like a casino. But quieter."

Sam smiled. "Yes, I do like the offices myself."

"Do you spend a lot of time at work?" said Ian. "I keep hearing about how busy lawyers are."

"Some," said Sam. "Work needs to be finished, and I don't go home till it's all done."

"I guess that's why you're single," said Ian. "I've been reading some dating advice books, and they all say that women don't like men who are always working late."

Sam looked at Ian and held up his left hand. "I'm not single. I'm married."

"Oh," said Ian, looking surprised. "I hadn't noticed your wedding band. My bad."

"That's okay."

"It's just that," Ian continued, "you've got those really natural hair plugs."

"Uh..." Sam glanced at me, looking unsure of how to respond.

"They *are* plugs, aren't they?" said Ian.

"Uh, yes, actually, they are. How could you tell?"

Ian shrugged. "I looked into getting plugs myself."

Sam and I stared at Ian, bug-eyed. His hair was big, curly, and threatened to overwhelm the rest of his face.

"You don't need plugs," I said. "What you need is a proper haircut."

"No, no," said Ian. "All the men in my family go bald at thirty-five. It's like someone flips a switch, and they go from hair to no hair overnight. So, I've researched plugs ahead of time. As soon as my switch gets flipped, I'm gonna get plugs. It's harder to get girls if you're bald. I mean, I wouldn't bother getting plugs if I was married, because I don't suppose my wife would care much. I've never heard of married men getting plugs. It's always the divorced and single men."

Ian looked at Sam inquisitively, and I wondered if his theory of men caring more about their looks if they were single was true. I was certainly aware of the stereotype of people letting themselves go when they were in a committed relationship.

There was a certain forced politeness in Sam's eyes now. He clearly didn't like Ian's picking up on his hair plugs, and he said, "I have to do it for the clients. They need a certain image."

"I wouldn't mind a bald lawyer," said Ian. "Would you, Tiff?"

"Uh..." I wasn't sure what to say.

The phone on Sam's desk rang, and he stabbed a button and put it on speakerphone. "Yes?"

The receptionist's voice floated over. "I'm sorry, but Mrs. Vanwilt is here a little early. She's heading toward your office—did you want me to ask her to wait?"

"No, I'll see her now," said Sam. "Wouldn't be right to make her wait."

When he hung up and looked at me, the relief in his eyes was unmistakable. "She's an important client. We'll have to end our chat early."

I nodded, wondering if I should apologize for Ian. "We had a few more questions..."

"You can ask Rob, I'm sure he knows everything I do." Sam stood up, indicating that the interview was over.

We shook hands politely, and I handed him my card with my usual spiel about calling me if he thought of anything. Sam smiled and nodded politely, but he clearly couldn't get rid of us soon enough.

As we headed out of his office, we walked past his client, a slightly chubby blonde woman in her late forties. Her hair was perfectly styled, her makeup immaculate, and she wore what was obviously a designer dress. Perhaps she really was a demanding high-paying client who Sam didn't want to keep waiting.

"That was kind of rude," said Ian, "the way Sam

basically kicked us out. He's probably got something to hide."

"Yeah, like the details of his plastic surgery. Why'd you have to go and ask him about his hair plugs? That obviously annoyed him."

Ian shrugged. "I was going to ask him where he got them done. His hair looks pretty good."

"Maybe next time," I said distractedly as I knocked on the door to Rob's office. "Although Sam might not agree to see us another time. He's probably scared you'll ask about his Botox next."

Rob Cornelison's office was a tad smaller than Sam's but had the air of opulence and success. The furniture was dark and comfy-looking, a large painting hung on one wall, and another wall consisted entirely of floor-to-ceiling windows that looked out on the Expressway.

If Sam was well-groomed and good looking, Rob was his opposite. Rob was half a head taller than me, about twice as wide as me, and had a shiny, hairless head. His skin hung in soft, pasty folds, there was a food stain on his white shirt, and his gray eyes were thoughtful and watery.

After we exchanged greetings and sat down on opposite sides of his large mahogany desk, Ian said, "Wow, you're really different from Sam!"

I stifled my cluck of irritation, but before I could apologize for Ian, Rob smiled and said, "I get that a lot! It takes all kinds to make a team."

I was taken aback by Rob's mellowness and said, "How are you different?"

"Oh, we look different, of course, there's that. If we've got a female client, she'd rather deal with Sam than me. I'm an ideas person, and Rob's more into details. Claudia's a bit of both, so it all works out."

I nodded. "Claudia is your other partner?"

"Exactly! Didn't Sam give you a list of all employees?"

"Er—no. We had to cut the interview a little short." I glanced at Ian, but he didn't seem to think the abrupt goodbye Sam had given us was his fault.

"I'll print out a list for you," said Rob. "We gave one to the police. Do you really think they missed something?"

Rob's question was guileless enough, but it's my policy never to rule out someone as a suspect. So, I shrugged and said, "Maybe. Who knows—it's happened before and it might've happened with Ella."

"I talked to Ella's sister," said Rob. "She seems to think Ronan Hastings had something to do with it all, but I doubt it. I wasn't on the Ronan case, of course, but I know the man through a friend of a friend—he's got it all together. He'd never do anything that could jeopardize his career. He seems like the crazy partying type, but he's actually very cautious and pragmatic."

"Mm-hmm," I said noncommittally. "What else do you know about Ronan?"

"Oh, not much." Rob handed us the employees' list and leaned back in his chair. "I met him once or twice. And I heard about him through my friend, of course. But I've never dealt with him in court—that was all Sam and Ella. They were on the case together."

Ian said, "Did Sam and Ella work together a lot?"

"Sure. Ella was a smart kid, worked on a lot of our high-profile cases. Most of the time she was partnered with Sam, but Claudia worked with her on a couple of cases over the last few months."

"And you?"

"No, I usually deal with divorce cases, and the associates I work with mostly are Keith and David. Ella worked on a lot of the litigation and financial assets cases."

"So, associates tend to get teamed up with the partners?"

"Not all the time. First-years do mostly paperwork. After a while they team up with senior people, not just partners. We've got a lot of people here."

"Who did Ella work with during the last few months?"

"Now that I think about it, mostly with Sam, and a couple of cases with Claudia. We try to rotate associates so they all get a chance to gain different kinds of experience, but Ella worked on some big projects recently. She was a great associate, very hardworking."

I nodded. "And she hadn't shown any unusual behavior in the last few months?"

"No, not that I'm aware of."

"And she wasn't stressed out about work? Maybe worried about getting fired?"

Rob looked surprised. "No. Ella was doing well. She was in line for a promotion, depending on which of the associates performed best. We could only promote one person, of course, but Ella was short-listed."

"And she knew that?"

"It was pretty obvious," said Rob. "Ella kept getting good projects."

"Who was her competition for the promotion?"

"Anyone could get it if they did well enough. But

we were looking at Keith Jols, Isaac Goldman and Terry Cooke."

I nodded. It was unlikely that anyone would commit murder over a promotion, but if there had been rumors about possible layoffs, perhaps someone had gotten jealous of the good projects Ella was getting. It seemed like a far-fetched theory, but I needed to pursue every possible motive.

I was trying to think of what to ask next, when Sam knocked and opened the door. "Rob, I'm heading to that meeting now."

"I'll join you as soon as I'm done here," Rob said.

Sam looked at me and then at Ian.

"We won't be much longer," I said to Sam apologetically.

Sam nodded, and was about to walk off, when Ian said to Sam, "Tiffany thinks you get Botox."

My jaw dropped and I felt my cheeks getting warmer.

Rob burst out laughing, and Sam looked at me, annoyed, and said, "Is that all you two are investigating? Whether I get Botox and hair plugs?"

"I'm sorry," I said. "Ian just—"

"Is observant," finished Rob. "I told you, man, everyone can tell you're getting stuff done to your face. Why bother?"

Sam sent a withering glance toward Rob. "Not everyone likes looking like a slob."

Rob threw his hands up. "Hey, at least people don't keep asking me where I got my plugs done."

Ian said, "Where *did* you get your plugs done? They look really good."

Sam shook his head in disgust. "Did you have any more questions about Ella? No? Then I'll head over to my meeting instead of wasting my time here."

He stomped off, and Ian and I turned back to Rob.

"Don't mind him," said Rob. "He's under a lot of pressure these days. Lots of late nights and early mornings."

"Sounds tough," said Ian.

"It's just a patch," Rob said. "We're trying to keep costs low by having a hiring freeze, but we're a tiny bit understaffed."

I nodded, grateful that at least Rob wasn't offended by Ian's questions, and thanked him for his time.

Rob shrugged. "I hope you find the answers you're looking for. I know I couldn't help you guys much, but maybe Claudia will know something. She was kind of a mentor to Ella, being the female partner and all that. Maybe they were close, and Claudia can tell you something."

I nodded hopefully. Perhaps he was right; maybe Claudia knew Ella well enough to tell us something new about her.

9

Claudia Chang's office was next door to Rob's, wedged in next to the conference room.

It was about the same size as Rob's, but unlike Sam and Rob's offices, hers actually seemed to reflect a little bit of personal taste. While their offices had Persian rugs on the floors and abstract art that matched the décor, Claudia's office had a soft white rug and a large painting of a stormy ocean. The chairs in her office were upholstered with a cheery yellow-and-black chevron pattern, and a small marble bust of Plato sat on her desk.

She was on the phone when we knocked, but she smiled and waved us in. Ian and I sat down on the upholstered chairs on the other side of her desk, and as she wrapped up her phone conversation, I admired her taste.

Claudia was stylish in a way that many older women are—confident, and secure in her choices. Her lipstick was a bold red, her almond eyes were lined with a bold winged eyeliner, and her jet-black hair was cut to just above shoulder length. Her earrings were large gray studs that looked like some kind of fancy uncut gemstone, and they matched the chunky gray necklace she wore over her white shift dress.

"Don't worry about it," Claudia was saying into the phone. "It's not an issue. Not at all. I'll take care of you wherever I go, you can count on that. Yes, absolutely." She laughed, as though the person on the other end had made a joke, and said, "Yes, of course. No. Okay, we'll catch up soon. Bye."

When she hung up, Claudia turned to us and smiled. "Ian and Tiffany? It's nice to meet you."

Ian and I murmured our polite greetings, and then Ian said, "I like that bust on your desk. Plato. Most people have Socrates."

Claudia nodded. "Yes, it's interested how similar those two were and yet how different."

"You mean their philosophies?"

"That, and just overall."

"Like how Socrates drank the hemlock, but Plato fled when they tried to kill him."

"Exactly." Claudia smiled and looked at me. "But I guess you're not here to talk philosophy."

"No," I said. I was slightly surprised that Ian knew all this trivia about Socrates and Plato, but then again, Ian knew all kinds of random things. "We were told you worked with Ella a lot."

Claudia nodded. "Yes. She was a smart kid."

Ian said, "Rob told us you were a kind of mentor to her. Since you're the female partner and all."

Claudia's smile died down and her eyes flashed with annoyance. "He said that? No, just because I'm the female partner, that doesn't make me a mentor to all the female associates." She looked at me and sighed. "I guess I shouldn't be so annoyed, but there aren't that many senior female lawyers these days and there's still all kinds of prejudices. You must know what I'm talking about—are there that many female PIs?"

I frowned thoughtfully. It was a question I hadn't thought about too much. "Not that many, actually. It's not a very convenient job—you need to be able to work all hours and deal with all kinds of shady people."

"So you know what I'm talking about."

I looked out through the glass wall that separated Claudia's office from the open-space work area. There seemed to be an equal number of young male and female employees, but I supposed that in Claudia's day, things were tougher for women. Of course, things were still tough for women, in many ways. Claudia seemed to be in her late fifties, and I wouldn't have been surprised if most of the female lawyers at this firm *did* view her as a role model.

I said, "You're very successful, though. I'm sure Ella must've looked up to you."

Claudia looked at me thoughtfully. "Did she? I'm not sure..." She shook her head. "I know, technically I'm a partner at this firm, but it's been a long grind. I'm not sure I'm someone to look up to."

There was a thoughtfulness to her voice that made it obvious she wasn't just being modest. I noticed the lack of a wedding band on her finger and said, "You never got married?"

Claudia smiled thinly. "I never did a lot of things. Never got married, never had kids, never had a proper vacation in the last ten years. Sometimes I wonder if it was worth it—which is why I'm not sure young women should look up to me."

Ian said, "Not everyone wants to get married and

have kids. Some people would rather have an amazing career."

Claudia turned to him and said, "That's nice of you to say. And I guess I've been lucky that way."

I said, "On the phone, you said that you'd take care of your client wherever you went. Are you going somewhere?"

Claudia looked at me, surprised. "No. I don't have time to take vacations."

"Then..."

"It's just a figure of speech. My client travels a lot, so I thought he'd relate to that."

I nodded. "Do you have to travel a lot for work?"

"Sometimes," said Claudia. "But most of our clients are Vegas-based."

"And what about Ella? What kind of work did she do with you?"

"We handled a few litigation cases. I haven't worked with her in the last six months, though— she's been working with Sam, mostly, during this time."

"So, you didn't actually see her that often during the last six months?"

"I'm afraid not. I know Rob and Sam think I was a mentor-like figure, but we weren't close. Ella would ask me a legal question or two sometimes, and we'd make small talk when we met, but I didn't know anything about her that Rob and Sam didn't. You're better off asking the other associates about her."

I tried to hide my disappointment. "She never confided in you? Maybe told you something personal off-hand?"

Claudia twisted her lips in a half-apologetic gesture. "I'm afraid not."

"And you didn't—I know you said you didn't see her that often in the last six months, but when you did, did Ella seem different in any way? Worried about something, maybe?"

"No. If anything, she was very busy with work. She and Sam worked on some big cases during that time."

Ian said, "It seems like she spent a lot of time with Sam in the last few months. But he said he didn't know too much about her, either."

"We're quite work-focused," admitted Claudia. "The economy's not great, and we need to really wow our clients."

Ian and I exchanged a glance. So far, our conversations with the partners had gone nowhere. Maybe it was time to talk to the other associates—Ella had spent all her time working, so at least one person in this place must know why she'd been killed.

10

"**I** like her," said Ian once we'd left Claudia's office and were walking toward the associates' desks. "She's smart."

Ian and Claudia had spent the last five minutes chatting about Plato and Socrates, and how much Ian wanted to visit Greece. I had to agree with Ian that she seemed smart and hardworking, but I was still disappointed she didn't know anything more about Ella.

"She might not want to be anyone's mentor," I said, "but I'm sure Ella looked up to her."

"Maybe, but that doesn't mean Ella confided in her. It'd make more sense for Ella to confide in someone her own age. Another associate, like herself."

We diligently went through the list of employees

Rob had given us. Although there were a few senior lawyers at the office, Ella hadn't done any work for them in the last few months, and chances were slim that she was friendly with anyone who wasn't an associate like herself. Ian and I headed over to the open-space work area where the associates sat in small low-walled cubicles and worked on cases. We introduced ourselves to all the associates, apologized for the intrusion, and asked questions.

There were eleven other associates, and they all seemed harried and stressed. Five women, six men. None of them seemed too upset that Ella had been killed, and none of them knew much about her.

Ian was, as usual, in high spirits. As we shuffled from one employee to another, he gushed, "I love talking to all these people! Everyone's so different, and it's so much fun to meet them all."

I squinched up my mouth and didn't say anything.

But inside, I was grumbling.

Maybe I'm not a people person like Ian, but none of the associates seemed all that different to me. Okay, so one of them had long hair and the others had short hair. One of them lived with their parents; one of them had five cats, each with individual personalities; and one of them enjoyed watching

French films without the subtitles and thought that superhero movies were drivel.

But deep down, they were all the same person: overworked, and overwhelmed by a life they hadn't expected. There was a thinness to their smiles, and a lack of enthusiasm that betrayed how tired they were; tired that their careers hadn't taken off quickly after all those years of law school; tired that they hadn't gotten all those promotions they'd expected to have gotten by now.

I felt an odd sense of empathy for the harried associates. A while back, I'd been like them: frustrated with my seemingly dead-end job at the casino and the likelihood that things would never change much. And as we chatted, I felt a wash of gratitude for my work as a PI. Sure, things might get a little dangerous once in a while, but at least I could pretty much dictate my hours, and every job was different.

The trouble with talking to too many people, even if they're all quite similar, is that you need to piece together bits of information and try to create a meaningful whole.

"She didn't hang out with us all that much," was the common refrain. "The last six months, she barely came to any office parties, and if she did, she left early. She'd hardly ever come to our Friday night drinks, either. She didn't come that last Friday..."

It turned out that all the associates other than Eric had been at work drinks on the Friday Ella had been killed.

Ian would ask a couple more questions about Ella, and I'd watch the associates as they answered. No, said everyone we talked to, Ella hadn't been acting strangely recently—but then, they didn't know her all that well. Nobody was particularly close friends with Ella, but nobody said they disliked her either.

"We all get along mostly," said one of the associates we talked to. Her name was Janet, and she was a short, skinny woman with limp brown hair that hung just below her ears. Her face was devoid of makeup, and the bags under her eyes looked like a permanent fixture from weeks of late nights. "Even though everyone knows there are budget cuts about to happen."

Ian and I exchanged a glance, thinking about the conversation between Sam and Rob.

"What cuts?" said Ian.

Janet shrugged. She seemed to be in her early thirties, and she'd already told us she didn't have time for relationships or proper meals. "Nobody's sure," she admitted. "It's all rumors—that the firm's not doing too well, and that there might be layoffs."

I said, "Have any of the partners talked about this?"

"No," said Janet. "They wouldn't, would they? That would destroy staff morale. Everyone's already looking for new jobs, but there aren't any jobs right now. At least, not ones that pay well enough."

Ian said, "We heard Ella was up for a promotion."

Janet nodded. "She was doing well. Her and Keith—one of them would've been promoted. None of the rest of us had a chance."

"I'm sure that's not true," Ian said encouragingly. "I'm sure you're on track for a promotion, too!"

Janet smiled wanly. "That's nice of you to say. But I'm not. I haven't been put on any of the big projects recently."

"And what about Keith?" I said. "What's he like?"

"You know," Janet said thoughtfully, "he actually never seemed to like Ella much. I mean," she added quickly, "I'm not saying he hated her enough to kill her or anything like that. It's just that he said a couple of mean things about her once. Said she wasn't a nice person, and that she didn't deserve the projects she was getting. That he had tons more experience than Ella."

I frowned. "Did he?"

"Oh, sure," said Janet. "And he'd probably have gotten the promotion instead of Ella. I just—I hardly ever saw him talk to her, and he really did seem to dislike her. There's another guy, too, who I hardly saw talking to Ella—Eric."

I nodded. "But it's a big firm."

"No, I mean, Eric went out of his way to avoid talking to her. One time Ella actually joined us for Friday drinks, and when she sat down next to Eric, he moved away to the other end of the bar."

"Maybe he had a crush on Ella," said Ian. "One time in elementary school, I had a crush on this girl with really nice hair, and she sat next to me one day and I couldn't even talk to her. I couldn't even look at her."

"Yes," I reminded Ian, "but you were probably six years old back then. We're talking about an adult man here."

"I don't think he had a crush on Ella," Janet said. "He just seemed to be busy avoiding her."

"Why would he avoid her?" I mused out loud. "Maybe you're misinterpreting the situation."

"Maybe," Janet said. "But I don't think so."

Ian and I had already talked to Keith and Eric, and at the time, they'd seemed busy and unhelpful. We'd thought nothing of it, but we had three more associates left to chat with, and when we asked them specifically about Keith and Eric, all three of them agreed with Janet's assessment—that, come to think of it, Keith had seemed to dislike Ella, and Eric had seemed to be avoiding her.

So Ian and I circled back to Keith and Eric, to have another short chat with them.

Keith was tall, with curly black hair and thick-rimmed black glasses. He looked more like an intense artist than a lawyer, and when he saw us approaching him again, he narrowed his eyes for a split second. He immediately pasted a smile on his face and pretended to be happy to see us again.

"How's the investigation going?" he said, obviously trying to sound enthusiastic and helpful.

"Not bad," I said.

"Tiffany's being modest," Ian said. "We've learned all kinds of helpful things! And everyone here's so nice."

"That's good to hear," said Keith politely.

Before I could tiptoe around Keith's supposed meanness to Ella, Ian said, "Lots of people are telling us you hated Ella."

Keith looked guilty and laughed nervously. "What? That's ridiculous!"

"Is it?" I said. I tried to sound sympathetic. "You and Ella were both up for the same promotion, and from what we've heard, you were far more experienced than Ella."

Keith smiled modestly. "Well..."

"So, it'd be normal for you to dislike Ella," I suggested.

Keith shook his head. "No, I didn't dislike her. I mean, I'm busy and stressed with work all the time, so I might've been a bit abrupt. And maybe someone misheard what I said once or twice. But I didn't hate Ella. That's simply not true."

I didn't buy his story. Why look so guilty if he had nothing to hide?

Ian said, "It's cool, man. You can hate someone you're competing against for a promotion."

But Keith just shook his head again. "You're wrong there. I never hated her."

"A couple of people mentioned you said mean things about Ella," I reminded him. "That you said she didn't deserve the projects she was getting and that she wasn't as experienced as you."

Keith shrugged. "So I'm a little abrupt sometimes. That doesn't mean anything—I'm like that about everyone."

I wasn't so sure. If Keith really was "like that about everyone," then his coworkers would've mentioned it. I said, "But it's true that Ella wasn't as experienced as you."

Keith nodded. "I've worked here two years longer than her. I've worked on bigger projects with better-paying clients. I've had a couple of job offers, too. I could've left—I probably would've if I didn't get the promotion."

I frowned, and Ian said, "And now the promotion's in the bag for you."

Keith looked at Ian in mild surprise. "I guess so. But I never... I mean, I always hoped I'd get it. Since I'm the better candidate."

"The best candidate doesn't always win," Ian said. "In fifth grade, there was this teacher's pet who was a bully, but he got away with everything because the teacher believed whatever he told her."

Keith looked at Ian warily. "Are you saying Ella was a bully?"

"I didn't know Ella," said Ian. "What do you think?"

Keith sighed and looked at me. "Are we done

here? I didn't hate Ella, and I don't know anything about her death. I've got a lot of work to get back to."

I nodded. "I guess we should let you get back to whatever you're working on."

Ian and I headed out of Keith's cubicle, and I stopped myself from saying anything out loud, since the other associates might overhear us.

I didn't quite buy the story that Keith didn't hate Ella, but a mild professional jealousy wasn't usually enough to go and murder someone over. Perhaps there was something else that we didn't know about Keith and Ella's relationship—perhaps Keith had some other reason for disliking her. But on the surface, it seemed like the usual rivalry that happens in workplaces sometimes, especially when two people are competing for the same thing.

On the other hand, Eric's behavior sounded a little odd to me. That, coupled with the fact that he'd left the work party early on Friday, made him seem like more of a suspect than Keith.

Eric was in his late twenties, and handsome in a preppie kind of way. He had dark brown hair that was fashionably cut, a square jaw, and charming eyes. There was something about his manner that was happy-go-lucky, and he was visibly surprised to see Ian and me return to his cubicle again.

"You guys've been here a long time," said Eric. "I thought you would've been done talking to everyone by now."

His tone was friendly and teasing, and I smiled politely. "It's taking a little longer than I expected."

"Everyone's been really helpful," said Ian. "They told us that you left the work party early on Friday."

Eric looked at us, surprised. "Didn't I tell you that myself?"

"I'll have to check my notes," I admitted. Perhaps Eric had told us that after all. "Where did you go after you left the party?"

"Straight home," said Eric, sounding bored. "Just like I told the cops."

"People also told us that you avoided Ella," said Ian. "They said you pretty much ran away every time she approached."

Eric laughed, a fake, hollow laugh. "I don't think that's true," he said nervously.

I watched him closely. "Are you sure? It sounds to me like you might've had a good reason to avoid Ella."

Something flickered in Eric's eyes, and for a moment, I thought that he'd admit that, yes, he'd been avoiding Ella.

But almost immediately, the mask of politeness

covered his face again, and he said, "That doesn't sound like me. Ella and I got along perfectly fine. I wasn't avoiding her at all."

"You know," said Ian, "it's not a crime to be scared of someone or to avoid them for some reason."

Eric's eyes flashed in annoyance. "I've already told you guys, I wasn't avoiding Ella. Is there anything else I can help you with?"

The hint was obvious, as was the fact that Eric wasn't about to tell us if anything had happened between him and Ella. So Ian and I said goodbye politely and reluctantly and headed over to talk to some of the senior lawyers, just in case they knew anything about Ella that no one else did.

Unsurprisingly, it turned out that none of the senior lawyers had known Ella too well. None of them had worked with her in recent months, and they all told us pretty much the same thing—the people who knew Ella best in the office would be Sam, who'd worked with her closely during the past six months, and perhaps some of the associates.

Ian and I left the offices feeling rather dejected. We hadn't come across any damning evidence, and although Keith and Eric had seemed slightly suspicious, we hadn't been able to learn anything unusual from them.

"Perhaps this is just a mugging gone bad after all," said Ian. "Perhaps we're just chasing shadows."

I shook my head. "No. I'm sure we're chasing an actual killer—they've just covered their tracks very well. At some point, they'll make a mistake, and we'll find out what's really going on."

11

I stopped at the grocery store on the way home and picked up a massive tub of chocolate ice cream. Normally, my dessert of choice would have been cupcakes, but we'd finished all the ones that Ian had made, and I didn't think he was in the mood to bake some more.

I would have preferred to attack this tub directly with a spoon as soon as I got home, but Ian said that he'd bring Snowflake over, and the three of us would hang out in my apartment and think about the case. I spooned out two scoops into a bowl for Ian, and a couple more scoops for myself.

Ian brought Snowflake over as promised, and while the two of us sat around gobbling up our chocolate ice cream, Snowflake decided that she was in a playful mood, rolling around on the floor and chasing her tail in circles.

"She'd make a good dancer," said Ian as he watched her. "They should have a dance show for kittens."

"I think they've got a show in Japan," I said, "where they take kittens and give them tiny boxes to squeeze into."

"That sounds like a fun show," said Ian. "Although it's probably not as exciting as *Dance Party USA*."

As if on cue, there was a knock on the door, and I opened it to find Nanna standing there, looking at me expectantly.

"Ian texted me," Nanna said. "He said he'd be here. It's time we created that rehearsal tape. Time's running out."

I tried not to grimace.

In preparation for her dance audition, Nanna had come dressed in a flowing red dress and sturdy-looking red shoes. Her lipstick was a bright red, and somehow, her white hair seemed to gleam more than usual.

"You look great," said Ian, beaming at her. "I've got some music on my phone, and we can watch a couple of old *Dance Party USA* episodes that I've saved. Gavin told me that they like audition tapes that show all kinds of dance moves, so I'm thinking we should do a routine that has a little of everything. Some salsa, some hip-hop, and maybe some waltzing."

Nanna nodded sagely. "Maybe we should practice awhile, and then we can make the audition tape."

I glanced around my living room warily. "Where exactly do you guys intend to practice your dancing?"

"We can push all the furniture off to one side," said Ian. "We'll have just enough space to do a quick routine."

I grumbled a bit, reminding them that this was my apartment, not a dance studio, and why couldn't they rehearse at Ian's place? Or my parents' house?

"You know how your mother will be," Nanna said. "And I thought you wanted me to have a little fun."

"And my place has too much furniture," said Ian. "It'll take much longer to clean out."

I rolled my eyes and shook my head, but I could see that there was no stopping those two. As they watched a couple of minutes of *Dance Party USA* on Ian's phone, Snowflake retreated to her favorite spot on top of the refrigerator and began to lick her paws slowly. I ate some more ice cream, and then Ian announced that it was time to push the furniture to one side, and that I needed to help out.

Nanna stood on one side, directing us as we shoved the sofa near the TV and put the coffee table in my bedroom.

"This still doesn't look very professional," said Nanna. "But I guess it'll have to do."

Ian had chosen a Latin dance track for their audition soundtrack, and he began to play it from his smartphone.

"This is how we should break up the routine," said Ian. "We've only got one minute, so I think we should do it in three parts of twenty seconds. Part one, we can start with the salsa. And then, we can do a little hip-hop, and we can end with the slow waltz. That way, we've got the tempo going on."

"I was just about to suggest that myself," said Nanna. "But I don't know any hip-hop moves."

"It's easy," said Ian. "You just move your hands around like this. You're old, so you don't need to do any of the more complicated moves. I can do something like this—" He lifted one leg and shook it in front of himself like he was doing the hokey pokey.

"That doesn't look like hip-hop to me," said Nanna.

"It's the newest thing," Ian assured her. "Now let's get started with the salsa. Tiffany, you can videotape us using your phone."

I raised one eyebrow. "Are you sure that's a good idea? Don't most of the contestants send in professional-looking videos?"

"Gavin told me it'd be okay," said Ian. "He said the producers just need something to catch their eye, it doesn't have to be all that polished."

Nanna and I exchanged a glance, her looking excited, me looking wary. I wasn't entirely sure that their idea of entering this dance show was a particularly good one, but I didn't want them to be too disappointed.

"Everything's different these days," Nanna said to me. "In our day, we didn't even have reality TV shows. Aren't they wonderful?"

I smiled and nodded, even though I wasn't such a big fan of reality shows myself. But Nanna's having fun was all that mattered.

"We need to start recording," said Ian. "Tiff, you stand there, and Nanna and I can dance here. I'll play the songs from your laptop, and we can put it on the kitchen countertop."

I stood in my position dutifully, and Ian set everything up the way he wanted. He told Nanna to walk forward from one side of the room and he would approach from the other.

"Tiff, you can start recording—I'll edit out the bits that we don't need. It might take a couple of tries."

I pressed record on my phone, and Ian started the playlist and began to prance forward from his side of the room, while Nanna did the same from her side. Both of them were horribly off rhythm, and I was pretty sure that neither of them could do the salsa.

When they met in the middle of the room, Ian held Nanna's hands, and they both began to sway their hips and step from side to side.

When Ian tried to move in one direction, Nanna completely misread his clues and started to move in the other. In the end, they both just kind of capered around the middle of the room, holding hands and swaying their hips. Occasionally Ian would let go of one of Nanna's hands, wave his own hand in the air with a flourish, and yell out, "Opa! Opa!"

I was pretty sure that the move had nothing to do with salsa, and thankfully, after a while, Ian decided it was time to move on to the hip-hop portion of the routine. He let go of Nanna's hands, dropped to the floor, and began doing the worm.

I turned the camera down so I could videotape him, and then I panned over to where Nanna was standing still, moving her arms in front of her face as if she was doing a very bad, geriatric version of the robot. When Ian got tired of doing the worm, he turned onto his back and used his feet to propel himself around in a circle, and then he jumped up and began twerking.

Nanna stared at him in surprise, and I did my best to hold in my laughter, afraid that the spasms rocking through my body would make the camera shake.

Finally, it was time for the waltz portion of their dance routine, and the two of them stood in the middle of the room and swayed back and forth. They were both barely moving and looked like they were exhausted and just killing time till they could go sit down.

When it was all over, Ian turned to me and said, "That must've been really cool to watch."

I looked at him incredulously, then glanced at Nanna, who was watching me hopefully. She looked as though she had no idea how bad the routine had been.

The two of them were clearly delusional, but for some reason, I couldn't bring myself to hurt their feelings and tell them how terrible it had been.

Instead, I said, "It was so *interesting* to watch."

"A couple more rounds, and it'll be perfect," said Ian.

Nanna nodded. "We haven't even rehearsed. I'm sure by the third time, the video will look really good."

I stood there, unable to think of a polite way to discourage them from entering the dance show, and videotaped them as the two of them went through their routine another seven times. My stomach hurt from all the effort of holding in my laughter, until finally, after the seventh time, Nanna declared that she was tired from all the exercise, and that she needed to put her feet up.

She sank down on my sofa, and Ian brought the coffee table out from my bedroom.

"This show is exhausting," Nanna said. "Maybe I'm too old for all this."

"No, you're not," said Ian loyally. "I'm sure you're a better dancer than all those other younger contestants."

Ian transferred the videos from my phone to the laptop. He said he'd edit them by tonight and email them off to the producers. We were just going to discuss how best to edit the videos, when there was a knock on the door.

I opened it to see Gavin standing outside, a hopeful smile on his face.

"I thought I'd drop by," he said.

I glared at him but stopped myself from saying anything too rude. If I hurt his feelings, Nanna and Ian might blame me for not getting a chance to enter *Dance Party USA*.

Ian peered at Gavin from behind my shoulder, and said, "Come in, come in. We've just finished videotaping our entry."

"That's great," said Gavin with enthusiasm that was clearly faked. He looked at me and said, "If Ian and Nanna are done with their audition, maybe the two of us can stay here and hang out." He raised his eyebrows suggestively, and I rolled my eyes.

"I was just leaving," said Nanna. "Tiffany, don't you have a shift to go to now?"

I shot Nanna a grateful look for coming up with an excuse for me, and nodded. "I do. Gavin, you'd better leave."

"I'll just stay for a few minutes," he said, settling down on the sofa. "I'm sure you've got a few minutes."

"She does," said Ian, and when I shot him a deadly glare, he quickly added, "But we need to spend that time working on Tiffany's new case."

"What new case?" said Gavin.

"It's a really important one," said Ian. "Tiffany needs to spend *all* her time working on it."

I walked to the door and held it open, and then I looked at Gavin, who glared at me and muttered something under his breath. As he left, he said aloud, "And here I was, trying to help you guys get on *Dance Party USA*."

Nanna shot me a panicked look, and I quickly said, "And we're all very grateful for that. If Nanna and Ian manage to enter the competition, that'll be great."

"Maybe the two of us can watch them onstage together," suggested Gavin.

I wasn't sure what to say to that. I didn't want him to have an excuse to sit next to me and grope my thigh again, but I did want him to try to nudge the producers in the direction of helping Nanna and Ian get through to the first round. Before I could say anything too rude, Ian said, "I'm sure Tiffany would love that."

"And I have to get to work on my case now," I

said. I hoped Gavin would get the obvious hint and leave—soon.

"Maybe you shouldn't work on so many cases," said Gavin. "Maybe your mother's right. Maybe you should work a little less so that you've got time for a relationship."

I rolled my eyes at him, but just as I opened my mouth to let him know that any relationship I'd spend time on wouldn't be with him, Ian began chatting about how excited he was to be entering *Dance Party USA*, and how grateful he was that Gavin was helping him and Nanna.

On that happy note, I said goodbye to Gavin and closed the door firmly behind him.

"If I never saw that guy again," I said, "I'd be perfectly happy."

12

My shift started early that evening, and as I stood in the brightly lit pit, dealing out cards to the blackjack players sitting in front of me, I let my mind wander.

Ella's death bothered me—as did the fact that nobody in her office seemed to know too much about her. Even if everyone was busy and competitive, surely at some point the co-workers would commiserate about their shared situations? Perhaps everyone in that office lacked that camaraderie, or perhaps for some reason, Ella was particularly unfriendly or avoiding her coworkers.

And what about Keith and Eric? I was convinced that both of them knew something about Ella, or had some kind of history with her—they just weren't willing to share it. Perhaps one of them, or both of them, had had an affair with Ella—in which case, their friends would know. I made a mental note to look up Keith and Eric's friends and ask them a few questions.

Then my mind wandered over to Ian and Nanna's audition tape. I smiled to myself. Their dance routine was truly terrible. It was the worst and most hilarious dance routine I'd ever seen, bar none. And I'd seen drunk bachelor party groomsmen doing the Macarena. I had no doubt that the two of them wouldn't get selected to audition onstage, and I needed to come up with some way of consoling them.

On my break, I checked the messages on my phone. There was a text from Ronan, asking if he could postpone our interview by a few days—the day after tomorrow was really not that convenient for him.

I sent him a curt reply—there was no way I was going to postpone our interview. He needed to make the time work, and if he didn't want to, I was perfectly happy to go to the press and let them know that Ronan had been lying about his alibi, and his involvement with Ella. That garnered a quick reply back from Ronan—he would make it work.

The rest of the shift passed in kind of a daze. I

tried to focus on the cards, but every now and then a hilarious image of Nanna and Ian trying to dance would pop up into my mind, and I had to stifle my laughter and try to concentrate on the players sitting in front of me.

The look on Nanna's face as Ian had started twerking had been priceless, and I imagined what the producers of *Dance Party USA* would think when they saw the video for themselves. I could imagine the staid, grizzly old producers doubling over in fits of laughter; I only hoped the video didn't get leaked and become viral and a permanent embarrassment for Nanna.

I was in a pretty good mood as I walked back home from my shift in the early hours of the morning. It was dark and chilly outside, but when I stepped into my apartment building, it was well lit and felt like home—cozy, warm and welcoming.

I unlocked the door to my apartment, flung it open, and was about to step inside nonchalantly, when I noticed the envelope sitting in the middle of my living room floor.

I froze. I'd encountered this situation in the past, and it was definitely not good.

I was absolutely sure there had been no papers on the floor when I'd left the house, and there were no papers lying around on my coffee table or kitchen countertop that could have floated over to the middle of the floor.

The only way an envelope could get to the middle of my living room floor was if someone had pushed it under my front door.

The last couple of times that had happened, the envelopes had turned out to contain creepy, threatening messages from dangerous killers who wanted to physically remove me from cases I was investigating.

My heart pounded loudly. The tiny hairs on the back of my neck stood up, and I glanced around.

Maybe whoever had sent me the envelope had also broken into my apartment and was lying in wait for me.

I thought back to unlocking my front door—the key had turned easily. There didn't seem to be any signs of breaking and entering. The apartment was silent—I strained my ears, listening for sounds of breathing, or maybe even quiet footsteps as the intruder waited for me. But there was nothing.

No telltale noises, no indication that someone else might be in my apartment.

I knew I needed to do a walk-through of my tiny place. I decided to leave the front door open, just in case someone jumped out at me and I needed to run away. I forced myself to walk inside quickly, before I could change my mind. I checked under the sofa, looked in the kitchen, and peered into my dark bedroom, cursing myself for not turning the light on before I left.

I couldn't see anyone. I flicked the light on in my bedroom. There was nobody standing there out in the open. I checked under the bed and behind the curtains, and then I flung open the closet, just in case anyone had decided to hide in there. I checked in the bathroom, pulling the shower curtain aside.

When I was finally convinced that nobody was lying in wait for me, I released a loud sigh of relief. I hadn't even been aware that I'd been holding my breath. But now I could feel the blood rushing through my veins, and I could hear the loudness of my own breath. I walked back to the front door, locked it, and then I sat on the sofa and stared at the envelope.

Perhaps it was just a flyer from a nearby restaurant, I told myself. But I knew that wasn't the case. I knew that someone had chosen to send me a message, and I wasn't sure that I wanted to open it and read it.

I thought briefly that perhaps I could avoid reading it now. I would have a good sleep, and when I woke up, I would read it. But I knew that if I didn't read it, I wouldn't be able to sleep very well. "It's probably nothing," I muttered aloud as I forced myself to pick up the envelope and open it carefully.

There was a piece of paper inside, and when I opened it, it turned out to be a typewritten message: "You should stop looking into other people's deaths. Ha ha."

I placed the piece of paper and the envelope gingerly on the coffee table and stared at them.

The note was particularly unnerving because of the weird "ha ha" at the end. What kind of crazy person sends a threatening note and ends it with "ha ha"?

I didn't like it one bit.

I stared at the note some more, trying to put myself into the shoes of a deranged killer who laughed about his threats.

The more I thought about it, the more annoyed I got. At the back of my mind, a little voice told me that Ronan must've sent me this note. He probably hadn't liked my insisting that we meet at our planned time, and now he wanted me to back off the case. I didn't know what he was hiding, and I didn't know why he would feel the need to threaten me if he was innocent of Ella's murder—but it must've been Ronan who had sent the note. I couldn't think of anyone else who would do such a thing.

Somehow, I forced myself to go change and get into bed. I slept fitfully for a few hours, and then I got up, got dressed, and texted Ian to come over.

Ian arrived within five minutes, carrying a frozen pizza that I immediately put into the oven. It was almost lunchtime, and I was starving.

I told Ian about the note, and he peered at it and frowned.

"Maybe this guy thinks he's the Joker," said Ian. "Maybe he thinks that threatening people is all a big joke."

I was about to rant and rave about people who sent creepy notes, when there was a knock on the door.

When I opened it, my heart skipped a beat, and I smiled.

"Hello, gorgeous," said Detective Ryan Dmitrou. "It's been a few days."

I felt myself drowning in his piercing gray eyes.

He looked as handsome as ever. He was almost too good looking to be a detective, I thought to myself. His brown hair was wavy and tousled, and his square jaw was covered with day-old stubble.

I wrapped my arms around his broad shoulders, and we exchanged a brief kiss before Ian said, "Hey, Ryan! It's good to see you—you're just in time."

I pulled away from Ryan reluctantly, and he said to Ian, "What do you mean, just in time?" He sniffed and said, "I guess you two are eating frozen pizza again?"

"Yeah," said Ian. "Did you want to join us for lunch?"

"I don't think so," said Ryan. "I don't have much time. I just dropped by to say hello to Tiffany—I was in the neighborhood, but I'm still working on a case."

"Well, we've got another case for you," said Ian. "Tiffany got a really creepy letter under her door last night."

Ryan looked at me, his gray eyes full of concern. "What note?" And then his eyes drifted over to the coffee table, and he narrowed his eyes. "Another threatening note under your door? Maybe it's time you got yourself some security cameras."

"Mr. Kaczynski across the hall won't let us do that," said Ian. "He says it invades his privacy."

"He's having an affair with someone," I said. "I can't risk annoying my neighbors, and having the apartment owners' association kicking me out of this place."

Ryan looked at the note and shook his head. "I'll take it to the station with me for fingerprinting," he said. "But you know how these things go. Even if I asked for a rush job, it'll take at least a couple of days."

"That's okay," I said, trying to sound braver than I felt. "I think I know who sent the note, and I don't think he really means business. He probably just wants me to stop looking into everything, but of course I'm not going to."

"Who do you think sent it?" said Ryan.

"Ronan," I said, and I filled him and Ian in on my text conversation with Ronan last night.

"This doesn't sound like Ronan's style," said Ian. "I still don't think he had anything to do with Ella's death."

I smiled cynically. "You're just a Ronan fan. Who else would bother to send me this? The timing's a little too perfect."

"Well, I'll take this with me anyway," said Ryan.

He leaned forward to give me a quick kiss on the cheek. "I need to rush back to work now."

"You are coming to dinner tonight, aren't you?" I said. "My mom still insists on setting me up with these horrible people."

Ryan grinned. "I'll be there. Although I don't think my presence will stop your mother."

"I'm going to be optimistic about that one," I said. "At least once she meets you, my mother is finally going to believe I have a boyfriend."

Ian and I had planned to meet Ella's best friend, Felicity, this evening, but just as we'd finished our lunch, Felicity texted us to say that she could chat with us during her lunch break. So Ian and I dashed out the door and drove over to the salad bar where Felicity had asked us to meet her.

The salad bar was housed in a squat terracotta building, wedged in between an insurance office and a hair salon. There were a couple of small law firms nearby, and I assumed that Felicity worked at one of them.

Inside the salad bar, it was all modern and bright and Scandinavian style—pale wooden floors, white-topped tables, and low-backed wooden chairs.

Felicity was already waiting for us at one of the tables, and she waved us over. She had a massive

Greek salad in front of her, and once introductions
were made all around, she dug into her food with a
fork, chomping on feta cheese and olives as we
chatted about Ella's death.

Felicity looked a lot more relaxed than the
lawyers we'd met at Ella's firm. She wore a dark gray
skirt suit and a white blouse. Her curly brown hair
was chopped into a stylish short haircut, and her
brown eyes were tinged with sadness when she
spoke about Ella.

"I was her closest friend," she said. "We'd catch
up every week or two, and we knew pretty much all
about each other's lives."

"You must've been shocked by the news," I said.

Felicity nodded. "I was. I never expected
anything like that to happen to someone I know."

There was no one else sitting down and eating
inside the salad bar, but there was a dark-suited man
placing an order at the register. I assumed that on
weekdays this place did a brisk carryout trade, with
workers from nearby offices grabbing a healthy
lunch to eat at their desks.

There was a short pause as Felicity gazed off into
space for a few seconds, and then she shook her
head. "It's hard to make friends in Vegas," she said.
"Most people are just passing through, and they're

only here for a few days. And when you work as hard as most lawyers do, you don't really have time to go out and meet people or make new friends."

"That's true," said Ian. "I never really made any friends here until I met Tiffany."

I grimaced. Most of my own friends were from back in my high school days, and many of them had moved away. But it was a common refrain—that people moved to a different city for work, and then they didn't have time to make new friends.

"People who move out here for work," said Felicity, "plan to move away after a few years. Vegas is a fun place for tourists, but it's not so much fun when you live here permanently."

"Most of the lawyers at Ella's firm told us that they didn't even have time for relationships," said Ian.

"That's true," said Felicity.

"Are you seeing anyone?" I asked.

Felicity shook her head quickly. "What the other lawyers told you is true. It's so hard to meet new people—you can't even make friends, and a relationship is just..."

"What about Ella?" I said. "Was she seeing anyone?"

"Not that I knew about. Of course, she might

have been seeing someone in secret and decided not to tell me."

"How about any ex-boyfriends?"

Felicity shook her head again. "I don't think Ella dated anyone while she was in Vegas."

"Maybe she was seeing someone in secret, like you said," I said. "Maybe she was dating someone from her work."

Felicity laughed. "That doesn't sound likely. Ella had a strict policy about never dating anyone from work. When she got her first job, she dated one of her coworkers, and it ended badly. She told me she'd never make that same mistake again."

I frowned and tapped my fingers on the table. "Did she mention anyone from her work to you? Maybe someone she disliked?"

Felicity munched on a tomato thoughtfully. "She did mention she was having a tough time at work," she said finally. "She said it was really busy, and that she was looking into something that she'd learned recently."

"In the Ronan Hastings case," I said excitedly.

Felicity shook her head. "Ella didn't tell me what it was about. Just that she'd learned something new, and that work was really busy, that she had all these projects on her plate. She was working with one of the partners in the firm, and she kept being put on very important projects. Of course, she'd also say that she was very grateful for those projects, because that meant she was likely to get a promotion soon. Oh—and now that I think back, she said she was competing against one other guy for the promotion —Cary or someone."

"Keith," Ian and I said in unison.

"Yes, that's it. She said this Keith guy didn't like her, and that he was trying to sabotage her chances."

I chewed my lower lip thoughtfully. "Did she say anything else about Keith?"

Felicity shook her head. "No. Just that he wasn't very nice."

I nodded. "And what about Eric? Did she say anything about a guy named Eric?"

For a split second, something like recognition glimmered in Felicity's eyes. But then she shook her head. "I thought the name sounded familiar, but I can't really remember Ella saying anything about Eric."

"Oh," I said, unable to keep the disappointment out of my voice. "We were told by the other associates that Eric had been acting strangely around Ella."

Felicity frowned. "How do you mean?"

"People told us he was avoiding Ella," said Ian. "It sounds like an odd thing for a grown man to do."

Felicity shrugged. "I don't know. Maybe he wasn't really avoiding her. Maybe it just seemed that way to some people."

I shook my head, unconvinced. "You were at home when Ella died, weren't you?" I said.

Felicity's eyes flashed with anger. "That's true. I was home. And you know what? For a long time the cops acted like I might've had something to do with Ella's death. It was really annoying—she was my closest friend."

"Why did the cops think you might have had something to do with her death?" I said, surprised. Felicity's affection for Ella had seemed pretty genuine to me.

"Oh, you know," Felicity said, lifting one shoulder in a half-shrug. "They thought maybe I was jealous of her professional success, or that we'd had some kind of argument. Just because they didn't have any other real suspects, that doesn't mean her closest friend would have anything to do with her death."

I agreed with Felicity. I couldn't see any reason to think that Felicity might have had something to do with Ella's death. And the lack of an alibi doesn't necessarily make somebody a killer.

"Do you think Ella would have gotten the promotion?" I said.

Felicity stabbed a piece of cucumber with a fork and held it up in front of her. "I'm not sure. I really hoped she would get it—she'd been working so hard. But you can't ever really tell with these kinds of things. One day you're the boss's darling, and the next day, they think you need to be demoted, or that a man would do a better job in a senior position."

"I guess things aren't going very well at your firm," I said sympathetically.

"No," said Felicity with a scowl. "It's not that I work any less hard than the guys—but when it comes time for promotions, it's always the men who get them. Just because I'm a woman, the Powers That Be think that I'll take off any day and choose to have babies, or that I won't be as good at dealing with clients."

"It's tough being a woman," said Ian. "I had to dress up like a woman once, and nobody took me seriously."

Felicity looked at him and smiled. "You must've looked like a funny woman."

"There was probably that too," Ian admitted.

We asked Felicity a few more questions about Ella—had she been acting strangely in the weeks leading up to her death, or had she mentioned anything unusual? But the answers were no, Ella had seemed perfectly normal right up till the last time that Felicity had seen her. Felicity couldn't think of anyone who might have hated Ella enough to hurt her.

"But there must have been someone," I mused out loud to Ian as we headed back to my car. "Somebody out there must've had a very good reason for wanting Ella dead."

13

On a hunch, Ian and I headed back to the offices of Elman and Associates to talk to Eric.

When we showed up, Eric was hunched over some paperwork. He didn't seem too pleased to see us, but he forced a smile onto his face and said with fake friendliness, "Don't tell me you've thought of something else?"

"Actually, I have," I said. "Can we talk to you in one of those conference rooms, instead of out here in your cubicle?"

"Why not?" said Eric with a wan smile.

We followed him into one of the empty conference rooms and closed the door behind us. After we all settled into comfy chairs, Eric said, "So, what did you guys think of, suddenly?"

The truth is, we hadn't really thought of anything new. However, it had occurred to me that if Eric or Keith knew something about Ella, they might be more willing to share that fact if we talked somewhere private—as opposed to somewhere like their cubicles, where ten of their coworkers could overhear them.

So I said, "I know you said you didn't have an alibi for the night of Ella's death, but I was wondering if you remember what you did when you were at home. Did you watch some TV? Perhaps some show that was airing at a particular time?"

Eric shook his head. "I was reading a book on the history of the Civil War."

"Oh." I scrunched up my mouth and looked slightly dejected.

I wondered what else I could ask Eric, when Ian said, "We've just come from talking to Felicity. Ella's best friend."

Eric raised one eyebrow. "Oh?"

Ian nodded sagely. "Yes. That's why we came here afterward. Felicity told us some very interesting things."

I didn't know where Ian was going with his bluff, but Eric's look of mild amusement tinged with politeness was suddenly replaced with one of wariness.

"Oh?" he said again, except this time, his voice was guarded and low.

"She told us everything," I said, continuing Ian's bluff. "So you don't need to keep it a secret from us anymore."

Suddenly, relief washed over Eric's face. "That's great!" he said. "I kept telling her there was no point keeping it a secret from the police, but she said she still didn't want anyone to know. We agreed that we'd tell people only if we absolutely had to."

I still had no idea what Eric was talking about, so I tried to mask my surprise by nodding and saying, "And Ella found out?"

"No, no, of course not!" said Eric. "She was one of the people we were keeping it a secret from. Felicity thought Ella might feel hurt for some reason if she found out the two of us were dating. I didn't see why it'd be such a big deal, but Felicity said we needed to be together for much longer before we told anybody else about our relationship."

Realization dawned. "That's why you were avoiding Ella—because you were afraid you'd blurt out something by mistake."

Eric nodded. "Exactly. I found the whole 'secret'

thing quite childish, and I wanted to tell everyone. But I knew Felicity would hate me if I let something slip out by accident, so I had to be extra careful. I was worried that if I talked to Ella and she mentioned Felicity, I'd look very happy or something, and then Ella would guess—and then Felicity would think I'd told people."

"Women," said Ian, in a sympathetic voice, "why do they want to make everything so complicated?"

"Maybe Felicity had a point," I said, suddenly feeling the need to defend all of womankind for our complexity. "You know how it is when people learn about your relationship, and then you have to break up, and things become awkward. Felicity probably worried that if you two broke up, Ella would find it hard to work with you."

Eric shrugged. "Maybe there was that."

We chatted a little more about his relationship with Felicity and how they'd met at an industry networking event and had been keeping it a secret from everyone they knew.

Now that I understood Eric's behavior, I needed to focus on Keith.

As we were saying goodbye to Eric, I said, "Ian and I are going to head over to talk to Keith now."

Eric shook his head. "You won't find Keith here

today. He's at an all-day onsite meeting with a client."

"We'll have to talk to Keith tomorrow, then," I said. "I know he's hiding something from us, and I'm going to find out what it is."

14

I hadn't wanted Ryan's meeting my parents for the first time to be a big deal, so I told my mother I didn't want her to invite anyone else over for dinner that night. However, Ian had begged and pleaded for me to take him along with us, and it occurred to me that Ian's being there might make the situation a little easier.

So that evening, I turned up at my mother's doorstep with Ian and Ryan standing on either side of me. Ryan had picked us up and driven us over, and he looked handsome in his white button-down shirt and khaki pants.

My mother opened the door and smiled at the three of us, exclaiming enthusiastically after I introduced Ryan to her, and telling us all to come in.

"It's so nice to meet you finally," Mom was saying

to Ryan. "I've heard a lot about you from Tiffany. It's too bad you couldn't come the other day."

"I was tied up with an emergency," Ryan said, "I felt terrible having to cancel like that."

"I know, I understand of course. The city needs more hardworking detectives like you..."

As I followed my mother over to the den, I could hear the words she was saying. But to my ears, it sounded as though she was saying, "I can't believe you exist! Tiffany told me about you, but I always thought she was making it up. You're not just an actor she hired, are you? I still can't believe my daughter actually has a boyfriend. I've been trying to set her up all these years, and she just didn't get along with any of those lovely young men."

Ryan chatted with my dad, who looked a lot less surprised than my mother to see proof of the existence of my boyfriend. A few minutes in, we all headed over to the dining room, and we'd just sat down at the table to dig into a delicious-looking meal of roast pork with carrots and mustard gravy, when there was a knock on the door.

"I didn't invite anyone else," my mother said quickly, "but I'll just go see who that is."

We all waited until she came back a few seconds later, followed by Gavin.

I stared at them, bug-eyed.

"I'm sorry, this seems like a bad time," Gavin said politely. "I just stopped by to have a quick chat with Nanna. I can come back another time if that would be more suitable."

"Nonsense," said my mother, rushing around and quickly setting another place. "You must join us for dinner. The more the merrier."

My mother turned to Ryan and introduced Gavin to him. "Gavin is a close friend of Tiffany's," she said.

"No," I said quickly, "that's not true. Gavin and I just met the other day. Gavin, this is my boyfriend, Ryan, the one I was telling you about—he's a detective with the LVMPD."

Gavin nodded and smiled politely. "It's nice to meet you," he said to Ryan, and I thought for a split second that he'd gotten the message—but then he turned around and gave me a broad wink.

I narrowed my eyes at Gavin, but it was clear he wasn't about to give up.

"Anyway, I just came around to tell Nanna—"

Just then, Nanna's and Ian's phones beeped simultaneously.

They both looked down to check their messages, and Ian let out a large whoop.

Nanna gasped. "It happened!"

"We're in!" said Ian. "We got into the first round of auditions!"

My jaw dropped. "*Dance Party USA*?"

"What else!" said Ian. "The audition's tomorrow —we'll have to practice a little in the morning, and then we're heading over to the studios in the afternoon! Can you believe it?"

"That's what I came over to say," said Gavin. "One of the producers texted me and said he loved the video you two sent in."

I couldn't seem to be able to close my mouth. What had just happened? Had Ian's and Nanna's video gotten mixed up with somebody else's? Or had Ian managed to do some kind of miracle feat of editing? I couldn't imagine a producer looking at the video of Ian and Nanna "dancing" and thinking they were good enough to be on the show.

"You look stunned," Ian said to me.

"I'm in shock," I managed to say. "I'm so happy for you guys."

"But why are you surprised?" said Ian. "Did you think we wouldn't get in?"

"No," I forced myself to say, "I thought you guys were very... interesting."

"I thought so too," said Nanna. "I had a good feeling about the whole thing."

"I had no doubt you guys would get in," said Gavin. "Congratulations! I'm sure you'll do well in the live audition tomorrow."

"Yes," I murmured, suddenly realizing that Ian and Nanna would have to perform live. What would they do when they were up onstage? "I'm so happy for you two," I repeated, unable to think of what else to say.

"I wish we could be there to watch you two," my mother said, sounding as though she couldn't quite believe they'd gotten through. "But we've already made plans with Bob and Patty for the whole day."

"Tiffany and I will come! We'll be right there in the audience cheering you on!" said Gavin. He looked at me and smirked. "Right, Tiff? You did promise me that we'd go together if Nanna and Ian got in."

I looked at Gavin and shook my head. "I don't think I'll be able to go," I said, not wanting to spend another minute with Gavin.

Ian groaned, and Nanna gave me a puzzled frown.

"Don't you want to come and see Ian and me perform?" said Nanna.

"Yeah, Tiff," said Ian. "You've got to come!"

I didn't see how I could get out of this, and Nanna's eyes looked so hopeful.

"Sure," I said reluctantly. "I'll be there in the audience, cheering you on. I'm sure you guys will do great."

15

When I got to at the casino that night for my shift, I was in a good mood.

I let the bright lights and garish colors of the casino floor wash over me like a sea of familiarity, and as I dealt cards to the players sitting in front of me, I thought back to the dinner.

Everything had gone quite well—my parents had seemed to like Ryan, and they'd chatted easily about his work, how he enjoyed Vegas, and what he thought of the New York Jets.

The only fly in the ointment had been Gavin; I knew he would show up to watch Nanna and Ian's audition with me. And I just knew that he didn't realize I wasn't interested in him, and that no matter how hard he tried, I would never get together with him. I had thought that if he met Ryan, he'd understand that I could report him for harassment and get him into trouble, but the truth was I wouldn't ever do something like that. So, I was stuck with him—and if he tried anything funny at the audition tomorrow, I'd be sure to put him in his place.

I fell into a light-hearted conversation with the three young men sitting in front of me, trying their best to win at blackjack. We talked about their holiday in Vegas, and what they thought of all the different casinos they'd been to. It turned out that the three men were old high school friends who came to Vegas together every year or two. This year, they were excited about going to a huge party that was being thrown at the Mermaid Bar. My smile faltered a bit as they talked about their parties; I tried to stay focused on the game and the customers sitting in front of me and not to think about Ronan.

But I couldn't help wondering about Ronan and his secrecy—did he really know anything about Ella? And if not, why had he lied about his alibi for that night?

THE NEXT DAY, Ian and I shared an early lunch together—microwave meals this time, rice with Thai curry—and then we headed over to Ronan's pent-house apartment.

Once again, we were given guest passes from the receptionist that allowed us to take the elevator straight up to the penthouse suite level. This time, when we knocked, we waited for five minutes until we heard the loud shuffle of slow footsteps, and then Ronan opened the door and blinked at us, bleary-eyed.

Today, he was wearing crumpled blue-and-white checked cotton pajamas, and his dark hair was disheveled and uncombed. Stubble covered his cheeks, and he smiled at Ian and me apologetically. "I forgot you guys were coming by. Come in, I guess I can't avoid talking to you."

I tried to check the annoyance that bubbled up inside me as I stepped into the penthouse living room area. Ian and I sat down next to each other on one of the white leather couches, and Ronan headed over to the kitchen area, where he made himself a steaming hot mug of coffee from his expensive-looking coffee machine.

The room filled with the aroma of delicious, rich coffee, and Ronan sat down opposite us, cradling the large coffee mug in his hands. In a way, I wasn't surprised that he didn't offer Ian and me anything to eat or drink—after all, he clearly wasn't happy to see us, and he wanted to get rid of us as soon as possible.

Ian said, "That coffee smells delicious."

Ronan smiled, clearly flattered by Ian's praise. "I got myself the new Gaggia Accademia coffee machine, and these are single-origin beans from Ethiopia."

"Tiffany and I only ever have instant," Ian said. "Unless we go out to have coffee, of course."

"The coffee they serve at most places is disgusting," Ronan sneered. "But I can see you probably don't know what good coffee tastes like, so let me make you a mug. I'm assuming you take cream?"

Ian nodded. "Cream and sugar."

"I'll make you a latte with one sugar," said Ronan.

I kept my thoughts to myself; I was torn between asking for a coffee for myself, and telling Ronan that we hadn't come here to chat about his expensive coffee habits.

But when he came back with a latte for Ian, I felt my annoyance subsiding. Ronan seemed to get a childlike pleasure from finding someone who appreciated his coffee habit, and Ian made appreciative noises as he sipped on his latte.

After a few more minutes of talking about coffee,

Ronan finally turned to me and said, "So, you're here to talk about Ella's death."

"I'm afraid so," I said, sounding apologetic. "Why did you lie about your alibi?"

Ronan shrugged. "You know, the usual. I didn't want the cops to think I had anything to do with her death, so I wanted to make sure I was busy at the time."

"But you weren't?"

Ronan smiled thinly. "Oh, I was. But it's not the kind of thing I can talk about in public. So of course, you'll have to make sure you don't tell anyone else about this."

I rolled my eyes and nodded. In my line of business, I come across secret affairs all too often—a young man or woman sleeping with someone they shouldn't be. I assumed that Ronan had a similar kind of secret. "I have to keep these kinds of secrets all the time," I told him. "Whatever it is you're up to, you can tell me. But I'll have to check your alibi."

Ronan shrugged. "That won't be too hard to do. I was here all night—I left the party early and came straight back. You can see me on the casino security footage. I came back at around nine, and I didn't leave until after lunchtime the next day."

I frowned. "Why bother to lie about it? Surely it's

not so embarrassing to say that you left the party early."

"Because there was someone else with me," Ronan said.

"Ahh." I nodded. "A secret affair."

Ronan laughed. "I wouldn't call it an affair—more like... a spiritual relationship."

I raised one eyebrow. "I'm sure that's a romantic way to describe it."

"No, it's not romantic at all," said Ronan. "That's literally what it is—a spiritual relationship. The pastor of one of the local churches visits me once in a while. He came by that night to talk to me. We had a long discussion about what it means to be a good person these days."

I stared at him in disbelief. Finally, I glanced at Ian to see what his reaction was. But Ian was busy drinking up his latte, and he didn't seem to be too surprised by Ronan's revelation.

"Why are you seeing a pastor?" I said finally. "And that sounds like a perfectly good thing to do. Why do you have to keep it a secret?"

Ronan smiled at me, his eyes glimmering with condescension. "Of course you wouldn't understand. But a guy like me, I'm supposed to be cool, I'm supposed to be hip and bad and dangerous and all those things—how does it look if I'm meeting with someone from the church, and talking about how to be a better person?"

He had a point. "I guess the gossip magazines wouldn't understand."

"Of course not," said Ronan. "They'd think I'd gone soft, and that my parties would no longer be as fun, and I'd probably start losing touch with my celebrity friends. So there's no way anyone can find out about this, you see."

"But why are you seeing a pastor?" I said, unable to contain my curiosity.

"Because I was in shock. I can't believe that girl got hurt at one of the parties I organized—I had nothing to do with it, but I didn't want that kind of thing to happen again. And I worried that it might. It's not my fault—but I felt responsible. I want to make sure nobody gets hurt. I just want people to have a good time."

I was speechless for a few seconds. I couldn't help looking at Ronan with a newfound respect, suddenly impressed by his dedication.

"That's a really good thing to do," Ian said seriously. "I think you can be a good person and still throw cool parties."

"Thanks," said Ronan. "But the media won't think so."

"You're doing the right thing," I found myself saying, "and I don't think it's fair you have to hide it. But I do understand, of course."

Ronan nodded somberly. "Thanks."

Ian had finished his latte, and he put it down on the coffee table in front of him. "Thanks for the drink," he said. "It was delicious."

Ronan grinned. "I know, right? You should get one of these."

"I might," said Ian thoughtfully. "Maybe I'll get into having nice coffees, like you."

Ronan stood up, indicating that our interview was over. "I guess I've told you what you came here to learn."

I stood up reluctantly. "I'm glad you had nothing to do with Ella's death," I said. "But I wish we'd been able to learn something useful. Are you absolutely sure there's nothing else Ella ever said to you that might give us a clue about what was going on in her life?"

"Actually," said Ronan with a frown, "now that I think back to that day in court, after I went up and yelled at her, she said something that seemed a bit odd."

My pulse quickened. "What?"

"She said she didn't need me to harass her—that she was being harassed enough at work." Ronan rubbed his chin thoughtfully. "At that time, I thought she was just complaining about how much work she had to do, but maybe she meant something else."

"Maybe she was talking about Keith," said Ian excitedly. "Maybe Keith wasn't just badmouthing Ella to other people—maybe he was being mean to her in person."

I looked at Ian and nodded grimly. "It sounds like something was happening at her work. We'd better look into the people at Elman and Associates again."

IAN and I headed home with a sudden, renewed vigor.

If what Ronan had said was true—that Ella being harassed by someone at work—then we needed to find out who the harasser was.

"It can't have been one of the other associates who was harassing her," Ian reasoned. "Unless it was Keith. Other than Keith, everyone else seemed to get along with Ella, and nobody said anything about anyone being mean to her, let alone harassing her."

"It might have been Keith. Or maybe it was one of the senior partners—just because they said they didn't work with Ella, or that they didn't know anything about her, doesn't mean that they were telling the truth. Perhaps Sam or Rob had an affair with Ella, or they were harassing her."

"Or maybe Claudia was harassing her," Ian added. "It's not like a woman can't harass another woman."

I nodded. "Whoever it is, we'd better find out."

16

Ian brought his laptop and Snowflake over to my apartment. Snowflake jumped on top of the fridge and started licking her paws vigorously, as though she never got a chance to lick her paws when she was at Ian's place, and Ian sat on the sofa and fired up his laptop.

I fired up my laptop too and logged in to my private investigator's database. Ian headed over to Google and social media and tried to find out if there was any publicly available incriminating information about the lawyers at Ella's firm.

The searches I ran on Sam, Rob, and Claudia brought up nothing. All of them were upstanding citizens with no records, not even a speeding ticket between them. Of course, why was I surprised? They were all powerful lawyers, and if they ever got into any kind of minor trouble with the law, they probably knew how to take care of it. I wondered if they had been just as good at taking care of more serious troubles—like a pesky younger employee.

I looked into Keith, too, but nothing interesting came up. He didn't have a record either, and the only interesting thing I learned was that he'd been living in Vegas for the last four years, having moved here from London, Kentucky.

"Did you get anything good?" I asked Ian. He shook his head.

"I've looked into Sam, Rob, and Claudia so far—all of them are pretty much ghosts on social media. There are a couple of news articles about them and the firm, but it's all publicity fluff. Hang on—I'm still looking into Keith. There wasn't anything interesting on the social media pages, but I can look a bit more."

"Everyone keeps their social media private these days," I said. "Let's just go talk to someone."

"Like who?"

I mentally scrolled through a list of names.

"Claudia," said Ian, before I could decide. "I liked her. She's smart and practical, and I'm pretty sure Ella thought of her as a mentor. If someone was harassing Ella, she might've hinted about it to Claudia."

"Okay, we might as well start with her. I'll call her office to make an appointment to see her."

When I called her office, I was told that Claudia was working from home. I hung up, disappointed, and told Ian what I'd learned.

But Ian's enthusiasm couldn't be dampened. "Let's go to her house, then! I'm sure she'll be happy to make time for us."

I shrugged and decided we might as well try—we had nothing to lose.

CLAUDIA LIVED IN TOOLE SPRINGS. It was a nice suburb up toward the north, family-friendly and pleasant enough. It wasn't as glamorous as gated communities like Lake Las Vegas, where the obscenely rich people lived, but I assumed that Claudia was being prudent with her money.

We drove up to the street were Claudia lived. Houses here were nice—double-story McMansions with fake arches and pillars, and manicured green lawns and lush green trees. Average households in Vegas preferred to keep their lawns desert-scaped to blend in with the natural environment, but people with a bit more money chose to flash their cash around by going green.

I parked three houses down from Claudia's, and Ian and I sat staring at it, wondering if she was even home.

Claudia's house was one of the few desert-scaped houses in the street. I thought it went well with Claudia's personality—she seemed like the kind of practical, hardworking person who didn't want to waste time and money on frivolities like a manicured lawn in the middle of the desert.

As we watched, the front door opened, and a tall, handsome man who looked to be in his early thirties stepped out. Claudia followed him, and the man turned around, gave Claudia a long hug and a kiss that went on for a few seconds, and murmured something in her ear.

We waited till he walked down to a red Toyota parked near Claudia's house and drove off.

I said, "At least we know she's home."

Suddenly, Ian gasped. "Hang on! I know that dude!"

I looked at him, bemused. "How?"

Ian squinched up his face. "Wait. It'll come to me. Wait...wait... wait... I know! I've seen him in that male revue, The Carpenters. You know, the show over at the Riverbelle."

I rolled my eyes. "I didn't know you liked that sort of thing."

"I don't. But one time, I met this bunch of girls who were here for a bachelorette party, and they told me they wanted to go to a male revue. So I took them to see The Carpenters. It was really fun, by the way. I mean, the guys took off their clothes and danced and all that, but the girls loved it—they all went and took their photos with the guys. They were all very friendly and—"

"Focus."

"Right. This guy. Sorry. Anyway, I'm sure he's a part of The Carpenters. I'll look him up on my phone, hang on."

So I waited, while Ian looked up The Carpenters. "There you go!" he said, thrusting the phone in my face after a few seconds. "Jarred Liano. It says here he's been with the group for four years now, and before that, he had a small part on the soap opera *Sands of Time*."

I knit my brows and read through Jarred's bio. Something seemed wrong with this picture—that Claudia would go out with a male dancer, after all her proclamations of not having time for relationships. Maybe none of Claudia's relationships had worked out in the past, because she had bad taste in men. Jarred didn't seem like the kind of person who'd want a serious relationship with a high-powered lawyer.

I sighed after scrolling through a few "tasteful" photos of a scantily clad Jarred. "Maybe we're judging too soon. Maybe Jarred's a lawyer on the side and male revues are a hobby."

Ian rolled his eyes as though I was nuts, and we stepped out of the car and walked hesitantly toward Claudia's house.

I knocked loudly, and Claudia opened the door within a few seconds. She was wearing dark slacks and a silky red blouse, and her face was lit up by a bright smile. When she saw us, the smile disappeared and was replaced instead with a confused frown. "Oh. You guys."

I shrugged, feeling kind of guilty that I wasn't her handsome lover. "Yeah. It's us. Can we come in?"

Claudia peered beyond us at the street. When she was convinced that there was no red Toyota in sight and her lover had not driven back for some reason, she smiled politely at us and nodded. "Sure, come in. I assume you are here to talk to me about Ella?"

"I'm afraid so," I said half-apologetically as I followed her inside.

Claudia's place looked as if it had been decorated by a professional who'd been instructed to keep things neutral and unfussy. The front door opened onto a small foyer, and the door to our right led to a small formal living room. Opposite us, the foyer narrowed into a hallway, and on our left was a door that I assumed led to the garage.

We turned right and followed Claudia into the living room. A dark abstract print rug lay on the floor, and dark leather sofas and an Andy Warhol print lent the room an air of comfy modernity.

We sat opposite each other on the leather sofas. There was a large leather handbag next to Claudia on the floor, and from where I sat, I could see files peeking out of it. I assumed she must've brought some cases home to work on.

Almost as soon as we sat down, Claudia's cell phone rang. "Excuse me," she said to us, "I'll be right back."

She answered the phone and walked out of the room, heading somewhere private. "No, this isn't a bad time at all," I heard her say as she walked out.

Ian and I sat nervously in silence, waiting for her to come back. A few minutes later, we heard footsteps in the hallway, and Claudia's voice speaking into the phone. "It's not a problem at all," she was saying. "Absolutely. You can count on me."

She hung up and entered the room, smiled at us, and then sat down opposite us again. "Sorry about that," she said. "I'm working from home today, and the calls never stop coming."

"I guess you can do other things when you work from home, too," Ian said, raising one eyebrow at her. "Like meeting handsome men."

Claudia laughed, suddenly looking a bit uneasy. "Oh, you guys must've seen Jarred leaving. He, uh, stopped by to pick up some papers."

"And yet," Ian said with a smile, "he wasn't carrying any papers when we saw him leave."

Claudia laughed and the color rose on her cheeks. "So sue me. It was nice to see him in the middle of the day—it's hard to make time for relationships when you're always so busy with work."

"Really?" said Ian. "What work does he do?"

Claudia looked at us hesitantly. "Uh... he's... um... a law student."

I raised one eyebrow. "And how did you meet?"

"He was there at one of those law student-practitioner dinners. We clicked instantly." She smiled, obviously recalling that night. "It was just over a year ago."

Ian and I exchanged a glance. I wasn't sure if she was telling the truth, but if she was, I'd actually been kind of close with my guess that he was a lawyer who danced on the side. Many students in Vegas have side jobs in the casino business.

Ian said, "Does Jarred have any hobbies?"

Claudia looked at him stonily. "What do you mean?"

"You know," said Ian, "like dancing, or entertaining women out on a girls' night?"

The annoyance left Claudia's face and was replaced by a look of exasperation. She rolled her eyes and sighed. "So, you found out he's in The Carpenters. I never thought you'd be prudes."

"We're not," I said quickly. "We were just wondering if you knew about it."

Claudia nodded. "He's smart, but he needed a way to put himself through college."

"Are you two... serious?"

Claudia looked down and fiddled with her skirt. "I'm not sure. I mean," she said, looking into my eyes again, "I haven't been in a relationship for a long time. I need to take it slow—I need my time to figure things out."

"That's true," I said, remembering how Claudia had previously told us that she wasn't seeing anyone. "And is that why you're keeping Jarred a secret?"

"Sort of," she admitted, "but also, people might laugh at my dating such a handsome younger man. They might think I'm a—you know, a cougar or something like that."

"It's not such a big deal these days if people think that."

Claudia relaxed suddenly. "No, I guess not. Anyway, I'm assuming you two didn't come here to chat about my relationship status?"

"No," Ian said, "we were wondering if you knew anything about Ella being harassed by someone."

Claudia shook her head immediately. "No, she never mentioned anything like that to me."

"You never saw anything suspicious? Maybe someone saying something to Ella, or her being upset sometime?"

Claudia shook her head again. "Nope. And if she really was being harassed, wouldn't she have complained to one of the other associates, instead of to me? Besides, she seemed reasonably happy with work."

"What about her relationship with Sam?" said Ian. "The two of them worked together a lot."

Claudia looked at us seriously. "I can tell you for a fact that there was nothing romantic between Sam and Ella."

"How can you be so sure?"

Claudia shook her head. "Sam's got his faults, but dating associates is not one of them."

"What faults?" I said quickly.

"Well." Claudia looked at me and hesitated. "This is all confidential, right?" I nodded. "The thing is, I didn't like his money habits. And I always suspected that he was trying to get me to leave the firm—we never got along. But Sam and Ella weren't that close, not the way you two are thinking. They worked together on a few cases. That was it."

We asked her a bit more about Ella. Could she think of anyone Ella had argued with, or had Ella seemed upset anytime recently? But Claudia couldn't tell us anything new, and in the end, when she got yet another client phone call, Ian and I thanked her and left her to her work.

After we stepped into the car, I turned on the aircon, closed my eyes and tried to think. Who else was there? Maybe Ronan had misheard what Ella had said; maybe she wasn't being harassed at work. Heck, maybe the whole thing really was just a wild goose chase.

And then, next to me in the passenger seat, Ian said, "Bingo!"

I opened my eyes and looked at him curiously. He was scrolling through his smartphone intently, his eyes sparkling with excitement.

I said, "What?"

"Look!" Ian showed me the screen on his phone, but then he turned it back before I could really see anything.

"What?" I repeated.

"I did another search on Keith," Ian said, his words gushing out quickly. "I couldn't find anything on social media, but then I found his email address associated with a comment he'd left on this blog post. There was a Gravatar linked to the comment, which was linked to the email, and I did an image search on the Gravatar. Turns out, that image's being used as the profile pic on an anonymous Twitter account!"

"Slow down." Most of Ian's words weren't quite making sense to me. "You're saying Keith's got an anonymous Twitter account?"

"I'm sure it's Keith's. The account handle is 'Honest Lawyer.'"

I hurried over to Ian's side and watched as he brought up the Twitter page. The account was

anonymous, and the profile had no other information that could be linked to Keith—but it was definitely Keith's account.

"I'm not surprised the account is anonymous,"
said Ian. "All his tweets are just him ranting and
raving about his employer—how much they over-
work him, how little they value him, and how he
should have gotten a promotion ages ago."

"Wait—what's that?"

Ian and I read the tweet together: "Hot female
lawyer might get this promotion over me—just
because she's sleeping with one of the senior
partners."

Ian and I stared at the tweet in shock.

"People did say that Keith was badmouthing Ella
behind her back," I said. "Maybe this is just another
way for him to downplay Ella's talent. Rob told us
Ella was very hardworking and intelligent. And
Claudia seemed really sure that there was nothing
romantic between Ella and Sam."

Ian scrolled down, and we saw a few more tweets
about this mysterious attractive female lawyer.
According to Keith's Twitter account, she was
sleeping with one of the senior partners—they both
always left office parties early, and they both often
worked late. In one tweet, he said, "I'm tempted to

tell the senior partner's wife about this affair—that would definitely get the girl fired. I need to get rid of her if I'm serious about this promotion."

I didn't like the sound of that tweet. I frowned to myself, and as though he'd read my thoughts, Ian said, "Keith really hated Ella, and he wanted her out of the picture. We need to get him to tell us the truth about what he did."

17

As we drove over to the offices of Elman and Associates, Ian and I talked about whether or not we believed Keith's tweets. Neither of us did.

"It's such a common thing," I said. "Once a woman starts to become successful, men start to talk about how she's only done well because she's sleeping with someone powerful. They all want to believe that successful women slept their way to the top."

"It's not fair," Ian said, "but I think you're right. Keith doesn't seem like a very nice person. I think he was spreading rumors about Ella. Maybe he tried to tell people at work that Ella was sleeping with one of the partners, but they didn't believe him—so he kept his thoughts to his anonymous Twitter account. Or maybe he was scared to spread these kinds of rumors at work because that would just get him into trouble."

When we arrived at the law offices, we found Keith typing away on his computer while simultaneously talking to someone on the phone. I wasn't sure how he could do both at the same time, but we waited till he finished his phone call, and then I said, "We really need to talk to you again."

Keith shook his head. "Can't you guys see how busy I am?"

"Trust me," Ian said, "you want to talk to us. You don't want us asking Sam or Rob about your Twitter account."

That got his attention. Keith's eyes widened slightly, and he stopped typing. His fingers froze in midair above his keyboard, and he slowly turned to look at Ian and me. His eyes were appraising, and within seconds, it was clear that he believed neither Ian nor I was bluffing.

"Let's go somewhere private," he said. "Anyone can overhear us talking here."

Once again, we found ourselves sitting in one of the small conference rooms, and Keith stared at us seriously. "How did you find out?"

Ian shrugged. "It was easy. You didn't do a very good job of hiding your tracks."

Keith grimaced. "Maybe I kind of wanted to get found out. I hate working here, thinking I have to work my ass off while some woman traipses to the top by sleeping with one of the partners. Life would've been so much easier if I'd been a pretty young woman."

"I don't think so," I snapped before I could stop myself. "I don't think you could stand two minutes of being a woman."

Keith looked at me wearily. "Whatever."

I tried to hide my annoyance, but I couldn't. I said, "Men like you always think that a woman who's getting ahead is doing that by sleeping around."

Keith shrugged. "I don't think that all the time. But Ella really was having an affair."

I crossed my arms. "Oh?"

"Look, it was obvious. Ella was sleeping with someone—she never talked about her love life, and she sometimes came to work wearing the same dress as the day before."

"All that means is that she had a boyfriend, or maybe she had casual encounters every now and then."

Keith shook his head. "No. It was definitely the

same person. She hardly ever came to office drinks or dinners, and she clammed up whenever anyone asked if she was seeing someone."

I tried to calm down and see things from Keith's perspective. "None of what you're saying means that Ella was seeing someone at work. What made you think that it was?"

"A hunch," said Keith. "Ella always got the good projects, and Sam was having an affair. A lot of the time he wouldn't wear his wedding ring, and he never took his wife on business trips. One time, I saw him kissing a brunette in the parking lot."

"You're sure it wasn't his wife?"

"No, his wife is blonde. But it wasn't Ella, either," Keith added quickly. "He was kissing some other woman. That was a year ago—I'm sure he'd moved on to Ella by now."

I pressed my lips together and tapped my fingertips on the conference table. I was starting to believe that Keith wasn't just randomly venting and badmouthing Ella; he really believed that she had been sleeping with Sam. But just because he believed that, it didn't make it true.

I thought back to the tweets we'd seen that had made us rush over to come talk to Keith.

"In one of the tweets," I said, "you talked about wanting to get rid of Ella."

Keith nodded. "I thought about going to talk to Sam's wife. But in the end, I couldn't do it—what would I say? I'd have to show up at their house, introduce myself, and say, "Did you know your husband is having an affair with someone at work?" She wouldn't believe me, and then she'd tell Sam, and then I'd probably get fired. I couldn't see that working out for me."

"Sounds like you made the right decision," Ian said. "Devoted spouses tend to kill the messenger. I think you would've gotten fired if you'd told Sam's wife. Besides, you had no proof he was having an affair with Ella."

"You didn't try anything else to get rid of Ella, did you?" I said.

Keith shook his head quickly. "Of course not! I didn't even have the guts to go talk to Sam's wife. What makes you think I would do anything stupid?"

I had to admit that I believed Keith. He didn't seem to have what it really took to sabotage a competitor, let alone go ahead and murder them. His actions were limited to anonymous ranting and raving, and the occasional grumbling and badmouthing at work.

"If you really want to know what was going on in Ella's life," said Keith, "you should go and talk to Sam."

18

I an and I pretty much raced over to Sam's office to talk to him, but his secretary put a damper on our plans by telling us he was out for the day—he'd be in tomorrow.

"But we can't make it tomorrow," Ian wailed, sounding heartbroken. "I have to go to the *Dance Party USA* audition."

"He'll be in the next day as well," the secretary said kindly, and Ian and I headed out and over to my parents' house.

"Nanna and I need to rehearse for our audition," Ian said, and I agreed.

I wasn't sure how their dance performance would improve with just a few hours of practice, but I knew it couldn't hurt.

When we showed up, we found Nanna and my parents waiting for us.

Nanna was in high spirits. She beamed at us and said, "We'll really wow them tomorrow!"

I exchanged a wary glance with my mother, who didn't look quite so enthusiastic.

"Are you sure it's safe for you to be doing this kind of stuff at your age?" she said to Nanna. "What if you fall down and break your hip or something? Hip replacements are expensive, you know."

Nanna refused to be annoyed and just laughed. "You could do with some optimism," she told my mother. "Look at me, I'm almost seventy-five, and I'm as strong as an ox. It comes down to mental strength, that's what it is. You need to try new things, and you can't be scared of a little dancing around."

My mother shot me a pleading glance, but I looked away quickly. I wasn't about to get involved. I didn't think this whole dance audition thing was a good idea, but it was nice to see Nanna so enthusiastic about something. The last few times she'd been so enthusiastic had been about "helping" me out with my investigations, and I was glad she'd found something that kept her distracted and not intent on meddling with my work. The way I looked at it, entering a silly dance competition was much safer for Nanna than chasing down murderers.

My dad and Ian pushed aside some furniture, and then Ian hit play on his smartphone, and music blared out. He and Nanna got back into the same routine—they swayed toward each other from opposite ends of the room, and then they stepped this way and that and gyrated their hips in some vague, not-at-all-salsa-like movements. As before, Ian insisted on throwing his arms up into the air every now and then and yelling, "Opa!"

"I thought you guys would open with some salsa," my dad said mildly, interrupting the music.

Nanna and Ian stopped with their strange side-to-side swaying, and Ian stared at my dad.

"This *is* salsa," Ian said.

But he danced as though he'd never seen a salsa dancer in his entire life, and my dad shook his head.

"Opa is a Greek dancing thing," he said.

Ian frowned. "It sounded familiar, and it sounds cool when I say it, so I'm going to keep doing it. Besides, what we're doing is fusion—it doesn't have to be purely salsa."

A laugh bubbled out of me unbidden, and I quickly turned it into a fit of coughing. Ian and Nanna looked at me suspiciously.

"Something got into my throat," I said apologetically. "Why don't you guys go back to your dance practice?"

And they did. One dance routine after the other, they went on and on, getting more out of breath as time went by. Their dancing didn't improve one bit, and I couldn't imagine they'd get any better unless they hired a choreographer and diligently practiced for at least a year.

Their salsa portion of the dance routine was not salsa-like at all, Ian's version of hip-hop was a disgrace to the dance form, and Nanna used the "waltz" portion of the dance section to basically stand still and catch her breath.

By the end of the hour, my dad had had a few suspicious coughing fits as well, and my mother looked stern and grim-faced.

"I think we've done enough practice," Nana said finally. "We don't want to tire ourselves out before the big day."

"You're right," Ian said. "It's more important to show up feeling energetic than to practice too much."

I raised my eyebrows, keeping my thoughts to myself, and my mother shook her head disapprovingly.

"You're not seriously thinking of entering," she said again, her voice dripping with disappointment.

"I thought we'd agreed to be optimistic," Nanna said, sounding slightly out of breath.

"I am being optimistic," my mother said. "I'm just worried that the two of you will make fools of yourselves on national TV."

Nanna smiled and shook her head. "Why do you care if we make fools of ourselves? I'm too old to care about what other people think, and if Ian wants to make a fool of himself, that's his business."

My mother shrugged, as if to say, "I tried to warn you."

"Besides," said Ian happily, "I know we've got a solid dance routine going on. It'll be way different from everyone else's."

My father had another suspicious fit of coughing, and I said, "It certainly will be."

ALL THROUGH MY shift that night, I thought about Ian and Nanna's dance performance. They were truly terrible—there was no way to sugarcoat it.

I had no idea how they had gotten through to the

first round, but I was sure it involved some kind of mix-up.

As the jingle of slot machines rang out, mixed with the occasional joyous scream of someone who'd won a small jackpot, I tried to focus on the players sitting in front of me.

But it was no use—I kept remembering Ian's horrible twerking, and Nanna's awkward robot. Nanna had now gotten used to Ian's twerking, and no longer stood shocked and horrified; however, I was sure that the judges who saw Ian's twerking would definitely be looking shocked and horrified.

In an attempt to stop thinking about Nanna and Ian and what would happen to them at the audition tomorrow, I thought about Sam.

Perhaps Keith had been wrong. Maybe Sam hadn't been having an affair with anyone at all— maybe the brunette Keith had seen Sam kissing was his sister, and he'd just been giving her a chaste peck on the cheek.

However, I remembered Ian's surprise that first day when he'd learned that Sam was married. It was true, there was something about the vain, superficial man that gave off an impression of being footloose and fancy-free. Maybe he was having an affair with someone, but so what? That didn't mean he'd had anything to do with Ella's death.

Or did it? And if so, how would we get him to admit that his relationship with Ella had been more than merely professional?

Ian and Nanna had been told to show up for the audition at noon, so of course, the next day, Ian woke me up at around ten in the morning. I'd barely gotten enough sleep, but it didn't really matter, because Ian had come bearing gifts—a box containing six cupcakes from a new bakery that had opened next to Neil's Diner. He'd purchased one of each flavor—red velvet, dark chocolate, orange, lemon-buttercream, pistachio and apple-cinnamon.

I made us a mug of coffee each and grabbed the dark chocolate cupcake for myself. When I bit in, it was so rich and moist and chocolatey that I forgot about everything else for a few long seconds.

When I came back to earth, Ian was saying, "This coffee tastes terrible! I'm going to have to tell my lawyer to release some money from the trust fund so that I can go and buy myself a nice coffee machine. I could really become a coffee enthusiast like Ronan."

I shrugged nonchalantly and chugged the instant coffee I'd made. I didn't earn enough to have expensive tastes like that. I finished the delicious chocolate cupcake and decided to attack the lemon-buttercream one next.

An hour later, Ian and I had finished all the cupcakes in the box, and we'd talked about the case a little bit. Of course, Ian could barely concentrate on the case because he was so excited about the upcoming audition—and he just couldn't stop talking about it.

"It's so much fun being on these reality TV shows," he said. "I'm so excited! It's going to be so much fun, and our dance routine is going to blow everyone out of the water. I'm pretty sure we're going to get through the next round, and the judges are going to be amazed by our skill..."

Ian went on and on for a while, until finally, there was a knock on the door.

I opened it to find Nanna standing there, almost jumping out of her wrinkled skin with excitement. She was wearing the same red dress she'd worn for the video audition, plus bright red lipstick and dark eyeliner.

"How did you learn to do your eyeliner like that?" I asked, slightly surprised. She'd also drawn thick eyebrows and applied a skillful layer of foundation that hid a large portion of her wrinkles.

"YouTube, silly! I called Gavin last night and asked him if they do our makeup professionally, but he said they don't. So I watched some videos, and I did it myself. I bet I won't look too bad on camera."

I nodded, and Ian said, "Do you think I should wear some makeup too?"

I wasn't too excited by the prospect of having to put makeup on Ian, so I said, "Don't you remember how horrible you looked when I had to put makeup on you so you could pretend to be a woman?"

"That's not what I meant," said Ian. "You know how all these movie actors wear makeup so they look better on screen—the camera makes you look all pale and old. I should probably put on some foundation and eyeliner, maybe a little mascara."

"You'll be fine," said Nanna quickly. "I don't want you going around stealing my thunder."

Ian nodded. "There's that, too. I wouldn't want to do that. You're the star."

The two of them spent half an hour practicing their dance routine—which meant that they went through the whole one-minute routine once, and then Ian insisted on practicing just the hip-hop section a few times. Nanna didn't mind that too much, since she mostly just stood there and waved her arms in the air stiffly, and I tried not to roll my eyes or laugh out loud as I watched them.

When we were about to head out, Ian turned to me and said, "What you think, Tiff? Don't we look amazing?"

They looked something.

"You…" I tried to think fast. Finally, I said, "I think you'll make the judges' jaws drop."

Gavin had told Nanna the address to go to, and when I turned up, it turned out to be a small conference room just west of McCarran Airport. There were signs announcing the *Dance Party USA* auditions, and we followed them to a small auditorium. At the door, a young man with a headset and clipboard told Nanna and Ian to go down the stairs and off to the left, and he told me to join the small group of twenty or so people sitting in the chairs facing the stage.

Most of the audience looked like parents or siblings of the contestants, and I found myself sitting in the back row, wondering how long the audition would take.

Unfortunately, a few minutes later, Gavin realized that I'd arrived, and he materialized at my side.

"I'm glad you came," he said. "I've been wanting to spend some more time with you."

He snaked an arm across the back of my chair, and I leaned forward so that I wouldn't have any contact with him.

"I'm just here to watch Nanna and Ian," I said. "I didn't want to let them down."

Gavin laughed. "You don't need to worry about letting them down—the only reason they got into the first round was that the producers thought they would be hilarious. Your nanna might even fall down during one of the routines, or Ian might break his arm doing the worm. They are going to do the same dance routine, aren't they?"

I looked at him through narrowed eyes. "You mean Nanna and Ian are just here to make fools of themselves?"

Gavin continued to grin like an idiot. "Of course. Every reality TV show needs the joker. Your nanna and Ian are the jokers for this show."

I continued to stare at him icily, and he mistook my frostiness for surprise.

"The shows need all kinds of characters," he went on. "You need someone that everyone hates, and you need the nice person, and you need the idiot, and you need—"

"Excuse me," I said, interrupting him and

rushing down the stairs in the direction I'd seen Nanna and Ian go.

A burly, wide-set man wearing a black suit and a headset stopped me. "Are you a contestant?"

"No," I said, "but I need to talk to—"

"If you're not a contestant, I can't let you through."

"But my nanna and my friend Ian are contestants, and I really need to talk to them," I said desperately.

The man shook his head. "If you need to talk to them, give them a phone call."

He didn't seem all that smart, but I couldn't really blame him for doing his job.

When I pulled out my cell phone, there weren't any bars. I rushed outside, where there was reception, and I dialed Ian's cell phone, praying that he would answer in time.

He did, sounding surprised that I'd called him.

"We're going onstage in a few minutes," Ian said. "I can't chat with you right now."

"This isn't a chat," I said. "I just talked to Gavin. He says the only reason you and Nanna are here at the audition is so that you can give the viewers something to laugh about. You're basically just going to go onstage to make fools of yourself."

I could almost see Ian frowning at the other end of the line. But when he finally spoke, all he said was, "So?"

"Don't you care? You and Nanna are going to look like idiots."

"I don't really care," Ian said nonchalantly. "I'm just here to have some fun, and if people think we're funny, then good for us. It's hard to be funny. And Nanna and I are having a good time—that's what really matters."

"Nanna might not feel the same way as you."

"I'll ask her."

I heard muffled voices, and then Ian came back on the line. "She says that's fine. If anything, we should probably ham it up. I mean, I was hoping to become, like, a world-renowned dancer or something, but if I'm just going to be the funny guy who also has good dance moves, that's good enough for me. And Nanna thinks so too—she's excited to be here, and we don't want you trying to bring us down."

I shook my head, even though Ian couldn't see me. "Well, don't do anything too stupid."

19

Although Ian had said that they'd be going onstage in a few minutes, it seemed to take forever.

There were three judges, the same people we'd seen on TV the other day—Francine, Carlos and Scott.

Then a presenter came onstage and talked about the show, how excited they were to be here in Vegas, and how talented all the contestants were. And then, finally, the contestants started to come onstage.

There were at least six couples who came onstage before Ian and Nanna. We didn't know if any of them got through to the next round or not, because the presenter told us that would be decided in a few days' time. The show would be edited to make it look like the judges' decisions had been instantaneous.

It took Nanna and Ian much longer than I'd expected to go onstage, but at least Gavin hadn't tried to manhandle me, and the silence needed for recording meant that he didn't bother to try to talk to me. Things weren't going too badly, so far.

When Nanna and Ian went on, there was a smattering of polite applause, and then they started their routine.

As the duo danced, I looked at the judges' faces —they must not have been told that Ian and Nanna were supposed to be the show's jokers. They stared at Ian and Nanna in disbelief, their jaws almost hitting the floor. At one point, Francine began to laugh so hard that she leaned back in her chair. She grabbed her concave stomach and leaned weakly against Carlos, who was sitting next to her.

I heard a few chuckles from the audience as well, and finally, the dance routine was over. Nanna hadn't fallen down or broken her hip, and Ian had managed not to trip over himself.

After they finished dancing, it was time for the judges to say something about their performance. The cameraman focused on Carlos, who threw up his hands in the air and made a face. "I'm speechless. I don't think I have anything to say to that."

The cameraman moved on to Francine, who was still weak with laughter, and she shook her head and waved her hands to indicate that she was laughing too hard to talk. Finally, Scott said, "That was a ridiculously bad performance. I think you guys are too far along the crazy end of the spectrum to need any advice. I'm not even sure how you managed to come up with that routine—it sure was entertaining, though."

Ian and Nanna grinned happily, pleased with their performance. They thanked the judges, bowed, and walked offstage. In a few days, we'd find out if they'd gotten through to the next round or not, and I could tell that despite the judges' comments, they were hoping they'd make it.

I was almost weak with relief that Ian and Nanna's dance routine was over. Perhaps I was turning into my mother, worrying about things that I didn't need to.

Ian was right—so what if they'd made fools of themselves? They were far from professional dancers. The two of them had enjoyed a fun time, and Nanna was probably excited to experience all the "glamour" of the reality TV world.

I was about to get up and sneak out when a skinny man wearing jeans and a checked shirt came onstage and clapped his hands to get our attention. "It's time for some audience reels," he said, "so if you could all clap and cheer loudly, that would be great."

The camera had turned to us, and I was stuck in my seat. For what felt like an hour, I clapped and cheered dutifully, anxious for it all to be over. It was almost time for my shift, and if I didn't leave soon, I'd be docked a day's pay.

"I think we've got enough clapping footage," said the man finally. "And now, if you've come with a loved one, it would be good if you could whisper in each other's ears, give each other a hug, or maybe even give each other a kiss."

I was about to get up and sneak off, when before I knew it, Gavin had wrapped his arms around my shoulders and started to pull me toward him for a kiss.

I shoved him away automatically—pushing so hard he almost fell off his chair. He looked at me in surprise. My hand flew up on its own and hit his cheek with a resounding slap.

I jumped out of my chair, wishing I could stomp on him like I would an insect, and said, "Don't ever try that again!"

As I stomped away from him, I heard the skinny man onstage saying, "Brilliant! Why didn't I think of that? Excellent fight footage! We'll make sure it appears on the show."

I didn't hear anything else, because I'd pretty much run out of the auditorium, but Gavin somehow managed to catch up with me.

"Why did you have to do that?" Gavin's face was taking on a shade of angry red, and I saw with some satisfaction that the skin on his left cheek was slightly pale from where I'd slapped him. "Now that's going to be on TV, and everyone will think I've made a fool of myself."

"But you were happy for Nanna and Ian to make fools of themselves," I snapped.

"Do you know how this could damage my career?" Gavin waved his arms about wildly. "Why don't you just act normal for once?"

"I *am* acting normal," I said. "Why can't you act like a reasonable person and take the hint? I have a boyfriend. I'm not interested in you, and I never will be."

I saw Ian and Nanna standing near my car, and as Gavin and I approached, Ian said, "I was going to text you. I didn't know if you'd be stuck in there forever, but Nanna and I are going to head home."

"I'm leaving," I said. "You guys did well."

"You only got in because of me," Gavin reminded us all. "Tiffany, don't you think that deserves some gratitude?"

"No," I said. "Keep your hands to yourself, and don't bother me again."

20

I made it to my shift at the casino just in time. As the happy noises and garish colors of the pit enveloped me in a warm embrace, I tried my best to stop my mind from wandering. I focused on the players sitting in front of me, trying to make witty banter, and I did my best to stop thinking about things outside the casino walls.

But it was to no avail. I couldn't shake my anger at Gavin's being so presumptuous, and the fact that I just couldn't seem to get rid of him. I hated that he'd known Nanna and Ian had been set up to look like fools on *Dance Party USA* and hadn't told them.

I was, however, relieved that the audition had gone pretty smoothly, and Ian and Nanna had managed to finish their short routine without hurting themselves. I was happy it was over and that neither of them had done anything *too* crazy onstage. I suddenly remembered Karma's warning that nothing good would come from entering the dance competition, and I had to smile to myself—for once, she'd been blissfully wrong.

And then, of course, there was the matter of Sam. The more I thought about it, the more I found myself believing Keith; it seemed highly likely that Sam might've been having an affair with Ella. And if he had indeed left the office happy hour before eight o'clock, like Keith had told us, then he'd certainly had enough time to be able to murder Ella.

As I dealt out the cards and laughed politely at a lame joke the player sitting in front of me made, I remembered the thoughtfulness in Sam's eyes as he'd talked about Ella. He'd really seemed to miss her—but perhaps there'd been something in his eyes that I'd missed. Perhaps he hadn't just been remembering Ella, his employee; he'd been remembering Ella, his former lover.

I gave myself a little shake. It was all speculation, unless I had some way to prove that he'd been having an affair with Ella, and that he'd had a reason to want her dead.

∾

I WALKED HOME SLOWLY from my shift, down the alley that ran behind the Cosmo Hotel, lost in my thoughts.

I nearly jumped out of my skin when a dark figure stepped out of the shadows and said, "Tiffany."

I was ready to scream when the figure said, "It's me. Johnson."

Johnson had been Stone's mentor at the CIA, and now he was the one helping us track down the man who'd allow Stone to come out of hiding.

My hands flew up to my chest and I tried to slow down my breathing. "Oh," I managed to say.

And then suddenly I felt a rush of excitement and adrenaline. "Any news about Tariq?"

"Not much," Johnson said in a serious, gravelly voice. "But we've tracked him to Santa Verona. I've got two PIs on the case—Mindy and Beth."

Worry stabbed at my heart. "Can we trust them?"

Johnson nodded. "Mindy is Stone's second cousin, and the two of them have a good track record. If anyone can find Tariq, it's them."

I chewed my lip, disappointed that Johnson hadn't shown up to tell me the good news that Tariq had been found; on the other hand, the fact that he'd been tracked to a small town and Johnson had two experienced investigators on the case was good news.

"Let me know if I can do anything to help," I said.

"I've got your number. With any luck, we'll find Tariq before Eli does."

The thought of Eli, the man who'd gotten Stone into all this trouble, made my heart pound loudly again. It was a race against time, and we needed to win it.

21

I got up in time for breakfast the next morning and texted Ian to come over.

I was munching on my cereal when he came by and started babbling about the new coffee machine he wanted to buy.

I wasn't interested in his coffee plans, so I interrupted him to say, "Have you talked to Nanna since yesterday? I didn't get a chance to call her."

Ian nodded. "I gave her a call last night to ask if she knew when the episode would air, and when we'd find out if we got through to the next round. She didn't know when it'd air, but she said we should know the judges' decisions by next week. You know," Ian added ruefully, "you didn't have to be so mean to Gavin. He might've been able to help us get on another reality TV show."

I let out an exasperated sigh. "Honestly, Ian! It's like you're becoming a reality TV show addict—except instead of watching them, you keep trying to appear on them. Aren't you sick of it?"

Ian looked at me in consternation. "What do you mean, 'sick of it'? I've only appeared on one show before this, and that was with you, and you stole the limelight."

"Because you went onstage and froze," I reminded him. "I didn't *want* to steal the limelight."

Ian shrugged. "Whatever. It's lots of fun to do these things. There's no business like show business—but of course, you wouldn't understand. You don't have Hollywood running through your veins."

I rolled my eyes, wondering where Ian had learned those clichés. "You're not trying to become famous by doing these shows, are you?"

Ian shook his head. "No, it's just that they're so much fun to do. The action, the lights, the cameras. It ain't over till the fat lady sings, Hollywood—"

"I get the idea."

"Maybe I'll ask Gavin if he knows when any more reality TV shows are coming to Vegas. Maybe I could get on one of those."

"What kind of show do you want to be on? It's not like you to get so addicted to being on camera."

Ian looked sort of embarrassed and shrugged. "It's not that I'm addicted to being on camera. It's just... it's hard to explain. It's like, for once, people are paying attention to me."

"People always pay attention to you."

"But this is different."

I shook my head, not understanding, but sensing that appearing on the show filled some kind of void in Ian's life. "I'm afraid Gavin won't want to help out much. He tried to kiss me yesterday, and I slapped him on camera. He said that I'd humiliated him and ruined his career prospects."

Ian burst out laughing. "Trust you to do something like that. But maybe Gavin will get over it— maybe I could introduce him to some girls, and then we'd become good friends, and then he can help me get on another show."

I looked at Ian hesitantly. "Sure, that might work. As long as you keep him away from me."

IAN and I arrived at the law offices an hour and a half later, and Sam's secretary told us that he was in.

When we knocked on his door, Sam peered at us through the glass walls of his office and waved at us to come inside, even though he was talking on the phone.

Ian and I headed in, sat down on the other side of his desk, and waited for him to finish his call.

"Now," said Sam after he'd finished, "how can I help you guys?"

His smile was friendly and obliging, and I felt a pang of discomfort.

Just because Keith had told us Sam was having an affair, that didn't mean it was true. It would be kind of awkward to ask Sam if he'd been sleeping with Ella, so instead of going ahead and asking him whether it was true or not, I told him how helpful his staff had been with the investigation so far.

"I was just wondering," I said, "did you remember anything about Ella's behavior in the last few months that might have been unusual?"

Sam shook his head. "I'm afraid not. We did work together a lot, but she seemed like the same old person."

I was about to ask him if anyone else might have been harassing her at work when there was a short knock on the door, and Rob walked in.

"I need to talk to you about the Morgan account," Rob said to Sam. He glanced at us meaningfully, and Sam shrugged.

"It's okay, we might as well trust them. They're private investigators, and it's not like they'd get repeat business if they went around blabbing about everyone else's secrets. Right, guys?"

Rob glanced at us again, and then he said softly, "I was going to pay the accountant's bill from there, but when I logged in this morning, there seemed to be less money than I remembered."

Sam frowned and typed away on his keyboard, clearly logging in to the account himself. A few seconds later, he pressed his lips together, and then he shook his head. "There seems to have been a few small transactions over the last few months. We must've been paying our incidentals from there."

Rob nodded. "That's what I thought, too. Just wanted to check with you."

Sam clicked his mouse a few times and said, "We might as well pay from the Citi account."

"The Citi account looks good," Rob said. "I checked it just before coming over here. We must've been paying some expenses from the Morgan account instead of the Citi account, but it's all good for now. We've got to streamline everything at some point."

After Rob left, I said, "What was that all about?"

"Nothing important," Sam said.

"Seems like you're short on cash," Ian said.

Sam scowled. "We're not short on cash. We've just got less cash in one account and more cash in another. It's a matter of choosing which one to pay from."

"The employees think that budget cuts are about to happen," Ian said.

"Maybe," Sam said, sounding guarded and suspicious. "Who said that?"

"Pretty much everyone," Ian said. "People think there might be job cuts."

Sam shook his head. "No, we won't need to cut jobs. If we just trim back some of our other expenses"—he glanced at the vase of fresh flowers that was sitting on his desk—"like all these flower deliveries, and all the free food we give to our employees, we can tighten our belts without anyone really noticing."

"You mean the employees here get free meals?" said Ian.

"Just free breakfast and snacks," said Sam. "You know, bagels, donuts, yogurt, fruit—that kind of stuff. I've been thinking of getting rid of all the bagels and donuts and yogurt, and just sticking to fruit."

"I'd notice if you suddenly got rid of my free donuts," Ian said. "I'd miss that a lot."

Sam sighed. "It was just an idea."

Ian said, "Claudia thinks you're bad with money."

Sam barked out a laugh. "Sure she does."

"Isn't that right, though, if you've got too many expenses?"

Sam looked at Ian warily. "Claudia and I disagree on things sometimes. But she's as involved with the expenses as I am."

"Anyway," I said, thinking that it was time to get to the reason we'd come here in the first place, "I was wondering—how long have you and your wife been married?"

Sam looked at me, seeming a little confused by the question. "Fifteen years now."

I nodded. "And... during all this time, I assume you've had an affair or two, here and there?"

Sam stared at me, his face emotionless and blank. "No."

"There's a rumor in the office," I persisted, "that you're having an affair with someone."

"That's not true," Sam said quickly. "I love my wife, and I'm completely faithful to her."

His answer was a little too fast, a little too glib.

"Did you go to the office happy hour on Friday night?"

"Yes, I already told you guys that."

"What time did you leave?"

Sam's smooth, wrinkle-free skin was starting to turn an unattractive shade of purple. "I don't remember. And now, if you'll excuse me, I've got to get back to work."

He turned back to his computer screen and began typing something on his keyboard. It was a clear dismissal, and I hadn't even gotten a chance to ask if he'd been having an affair with Ella.

Ian said, "It's funny how you got busy all of a sudden."

"I'm a busy man," Sam said. "And I've got a couple of important phone calls to make now."

He glanced at the door to his office, and Ian and I stood up, unsure of what to do next.

In the end, we trooped out, and as we passed Sam's secretary, she said, "Did you guys get all the information you needed?"

I stared at her blankly, and she repeated the question.

"Yes," I said, feeling like an idiot. I wished I had just come out and asked him if he'd been having an affair with Ella. But what made me think that he would admit to it? And then, I had a brainwave. I said, "Sam needed to make an emergency phone call, but he told us to get his wife's phone number from you."

Sam's secretary glanced through the glass walls of his office; as we'd said, Sam was busy talking away on the phone. She nodded and pulled out a phone number for us, which I wrote down quickly, thanking her and leaving before Sam could find out what we'd done.

Sam's wife's name was Nicole, and we were told she'd be home at this hour. I had no idea how much Nicole knew about her husband—I could only hope that she knew something we didn't, and that she'd be willing to share that knowledge with us.

Sam and Nicole lived in a large two-story house in Summerlin.

Ian and I drove over, and then I parked two houses down and called the number I'd gotten from Sam's secretary.

Nicole answered warily after three rings, and I introduced myself awkwardly, explaining that I was looking into the death of a young lawyer who worked at Sam's firm, and would it be possible to talk to her about this for a few minutes?

"I don't see why not," Nicole said, still sounding slightly suspicious, "but I don't think this has anything to do with me or Sam."

"No, of course not," I said, "but I was thinking there might be an off chance you'd met Ella even though you didn't know who she was."

"I don't see how that would be possible."

I sighed. "I know it sounds ridiculous, but if you're free to chat for a few minutes, maybe I could explain myself a bit better. I'm parked outside your house, and if you're free right now, maybe I could come in and ask you a few questions?"

There was a brief pause as Nicole considered the request, and then she said, "Oh, why not? Come on over."

Nicole answered the door within half a minute of my knock. She turned out to be a slender platinum blonde with flawless skin. Although she wore no makeup, her eyelashes were long and thick, and I suspected they were extensions.

Ian and I introduced ourselves, and then we followed her inside and found ourselves in a stylish, expensively decorated living room. Red Persian carpet on the floor, brown leather sofas, and an intricate landscape painting hanging on the wall.

Ian and I settled down on one of the sofas, and Nicole sat opposite us, watching us carefully.

"You have a gorgeous house," I said, trying to sound warm and friendly.

Nicole nodded politely. "What did you want to ask me about this woman's death?"

"I was wondering if you'd ever met her. She was a

pretty brunette, and I thought that perhaps you'd have seen her at work events or something like that."

Nicole shook her head. "I avoid Sam's work events as much as I can—I've got three small kids, and Sam isn't all that keen on my going with him to these things anyway."

"Are you sure?" I said. "I've got a photo of her right here on my phone."

Nicole crossed her arms. "I'm sure. I've never met any of Sam's employees."

We were getting nowhere with this line of questioning, so I said, "How long have you and Sam been married?"

Nicole's eyes were unfriendly and unsmiling. "How is this related to your investigation?"

I shifted awkwardly in my seat. I wondered how I could delicately explain that I suspected her husband of having an affair with the dead woman, when Ian said, "We think your husband may have been more than Ella's employer."

Nicole turned to look at Ian and smiled cynically, raising her eyebrows. "You think my husband was having an affair with Ella? And even if he did, what does that have to do with me?"

I frowned at the ease with which Nicole mention the words "my husband" and "affair" in the same breath. "So you knew your husband was having an affair?"

Nicole turned from Ian to look at me again, and this time her smile was less cynical and more sad. "I found out two years ago. I discovered some emails, and then I hired a private investigator to follow him around. I guess I found out what I wanted to know—he was seeing some woman, some young girl who worked at a café near his office."

"What did you do after you found out about his affair?"

"I thought about my options. I could divorce him, and then I'd be on my own, trying to raise three kids who didn't have a good relationship with their father. Or I could accuse him of cheating on me, he'd deny it, and then we'd have a huge fight, and our marriage would be even more difficult than it already was. In the end, I decided to be practical—I would overlook his indiscretion, and he would continue to pretend to be a good father and husband."

I stared at Nicole, half pitying her for her difficult choice, and half admiring her for having the strength to go through this for the sake of her children.

"Maybe he ended that affair," Ian said.

Nicole shook her head. "Every now and then I snoop on his emails and text. I know I shouldn't, but I can't help myself—he still texts this woman, tells her that he loves her and that as soon as the kids are grown up, he'll divorce me and marry her. Maybe he even means all that."

"Maybe the woman was Ella," I said. "Maybe your PI got some facts wrong."

Nicole stood up. "Wait here. I've still got the photos that the guy took for me—you'll know if it was the woman you're investigating."

She returned within a few minutes, a large manila envelope in her hand. She handed it to me, and I pulled out a series of photographs, all showing Sam with another woman—a woman who wasn't Ella. Sure, the woman in the picture had brown hair, but she wasn't our gal.

I shoved the photos back in the envelope and handed it to Nicole. "I guess we've just been wasting your time."

Nicole shook her head sadly. "You're right about his affair. Just wrong about who he was having it with."

～

Ian and I stopped for lunch at a fast-food place that was on the way to Sam's office, and as we dug into greasy french fries and burgers heaped with cheese, mayo and ketchup, we talked about Nicole and Ella.

"Maybe Sam really was seeing Ella," Ian said, "and maybe Nicole lied about the whole thing. Maybe she's the one who killed Ella."

I shook my head. "That doesn't make any sense. First of all, why would Nicole kill Ella? She's got no motive. Sam's still having an affair with this other woman, and she's still stuck in a loveless marriage. Even if Sam *was* having an affair with Ella, Nicole doesn't have any reason to kill her."

"Okay, so perhaps Sam was having an affair with Ella—and Nicole doesn't know about it."

I frowned and chewed a french fry thoughtfully. "I don't think that's the case," I said finally. "I think Nicole's right—that Sam is just with this one woman. I think this is the woman Keith saw in the parking lot. If Sam had been having an affair with Ella, Keith wouldn't have been the only one who suspected. The other associates would've gotten a whiff of it too—if Ella was slated for that promotion, all of them would have to be a little jealous of her."

"So, Ella could've been talking about any of the

associates when she talked about someone harassing her at work," Ian said.

"You're forgetting that they were all having drinks on Friday night, except for Keith and Eric."

"And neither of them seem like killers. But back to Sam—what if there was some way he was having a secret affair with Ella?"

"Ronan didn't say that Ella was having an affair with someone. According to him, Ella said that she was being *harassed* at work. Not that she was seeing someone, or having relationship problems."

"So maybe Sam was harassing her?"

I shook my head. "I can't quite believe that. He was having an affair with someone else, why would he harass Ella? Especially if he appreciated her intelligence and work ethic."

"So maybe it wasn't Sam," Ian said, his voice tinged with disappointment. I knew how he felt—for a few moments, I'd been absolutely sure that Sam had been having an affair with Ella, and that he'd killed her. "Maybe someone else at work was harassing Ella, and they're the ones who went ahead and killed her."

"It could've been anyone," I said dejectedly, munching on another fry. "We should go back and talk to Sam again. He wasn't the one harassing Ella, but maybe he knew who it was."

23

Ian and I headed back to Sam's office, and I could see through the glass walls that he was staring out the window, talking on his cell phone. Without waiting to knock, the two of us marched through the door, and Sam turned around and stared at us.

"I have to go," he said to whoever he was talking to. He hung up and said to us, "I'm busy."

I didn't wait for him to make his excuses. My words came out in a rush. "We know that you had nothing to do with Ella's death and that you weren't having an affair with her. But someone else in this office was, and we need your help."

Sam looked at us suspiciously, glancing from me to Ian as though he didn't quite believe our words.

Ian and I stared back at him silently.

It was an impasse, and after what felt like half an hour, Sam said, "What made you change your mind so suddenly?"

I shrugged. "I did some investigating. I'm an investigator, after all."

Sam motioned us to sit down, and he went and sat on the other side of his desk. "I'm glad you two have come to your senses," he said, but his voice was still tinged with suspicion.

"I'm really sorry about before," I said, deciding to go the groveling route. "I should've known you would never do something like that. But we were told that Ella was being harassed by someone at work—do you know if she'd been having an affair or was being bullied?"

Sam frowned and shook his head quickly. "I worked with Ella quite a bit over the last few months —professionally, of course, nothing else. I'd like to think that if something had been going on, she would have told me."

"But she didn't say anything?"

Sam shook his head. "Nothing at all. I find it hard to believe that someone was harassing her."

"Maybe she was scared of the harasser," Ian suggested.

Sam looked at him thoughtfully and nodded.

"Maybe. But I don't think anyone in my office would behave like that. We've got a strict no-fraternization policy."

"Some people don't follow policies," I reminded him. "Maybe it was someone powerful, like another partner." I frowned, wondering why I hadn't thought of this before. "Maybe it was Rob."

Sam laughed and shook his head. "Rob is gay. And I barely saw him even talking to Ella over the last few months. He definitely wouldn't be harassing her."

"Then maybe one of the other senior employees?" I thought back, wondering who it could be.

"If it had been a senior employee and not a partner," Ian reminded me, "Ella would have told Sam. She wouldn't have been scared to talk about it. It must've been one of the other partners—if not Rob, what about Claudia?"

"But Claudia is a woman."

Ian shrugged. "Women can harass other women."

We both looked at Sam, who rubbed his chin thoughtfully. "I'm not really sure about that. They always seemed to get along."

"And it couldn't have been Claudia," Ian said,

remembering. "She was at the party on Friday night, wasn't she?"

Sam looked at us seriously. "Now that you mention it—Claudia left the party early."

There was silence for a few long seconds as we each thought about the possibility of Claudia's having something to do with Ella's death.

Finally, I said, "We'd better go and talk to Claudia again. See what she has to say about all this."

"She's not at work today," Sam said. "She said she'd be working from home."

I said, "Again? We've already talked to her at home once, may as well go over there once more."

24

As we left Sam's office, Ian said, "I really don't want to believe that Claudia had anything to do with Ella's death. Claudia's so nice, and so intelligent!"

I shrugged. "People aren't always what they seem."

"Maybe we're missing something," Ian insisted. "Let's go chat with Rob. Maybe he knows something about Claudia that Sam doesn't know. Maybe he knows why Claudia left the party early."

Reluctantly, I followed Ian to Rob's office. When Ian rapped on his door, Rob looked up and waved us in with a smile. "How's it going?" he asked, looking at us curiously.

Ian let out a dramatic sigh. "It's going terribly!

We've been looking into Sam's affair—why didn't you tell us he was having one?"

Rob looked at us sheepishly. "I just—I guess I didn't see what it could have to do with Ella's death. I suppose I was trying to protect Sam."

"From what?" I said, sounding more annoyed than I'd meant to. "If he had nothing to do with Ella's death, us knowing about his affair wouldn't be a big deal."

Rob scrunched up his face. "I don't know. I was— did you guys just come in here to yell at me?"

My expression softened. "No, of course not. We were just wondering what else you know that you haven't told us yet. You don't have to protect anyone —just tell us the truth."

Rob sighed and rubbed his right temple. "What exactly did you want to know?"

"Start with Sam," said Ian. "What was the deal with this affair?"

Rob shook his head. "It was a bad idea all around, but Sam said he was in love with this woman. It's a big secret, though—nobody knows apart from me, so you two better keep it to your-selves. Sam was planning to leave his wife to be with her. Sam had absolutely nothing to do with Ella romantically," he added, glancing in my direction. "He was really hung up on Angelique."

I frowned and nodded. Perhaps Sam's affair had something to do with Ella's death after all—I wasn't sure what, but I decided to keep Rob talking. "And he really planned on getting a divorce?"

"He wasn't sure what to do," said Rob. "Anqelique had expensive tastes, and if Sam got divorced, his wife would get half his assets, which wouldn't do. He couldn't decide what to do, leaning first this way, then that."

"Couldn't he do something clever with his assets," said Ian, "like hire an accountant to hide them or something?"

Rob grinned. "I don't think any accountant's that good! Sam did mention that he thought about selling out of his partnership so that his wife wouldn't get her hands on the firm, but then he'd have a lot of cash and she'd just get that."

Ian said, "So the firm's worth a lot?"

Rob shrugged. "It used to be. But we've had a lot of expenses recently, and some of our old clients have left, so..."

His voice trailed off, and I murmured something sympathetic.

"Where does Claudia come into all this?" said Ian.

"She doesn't," said Rob. "I mean, Sam and I have discussed that if she left the firm, we'd save on expenses because we'd need to pay one less partner, but when Sam hinted at it to Claudia once, she said she was perfectly happy here. And I'm not sure Claudia even knows about Sam's affair."

"Claudia did mention that Sam hoped she'd leave the firm."

"It was just a hint," said Rob, "and one that she shot down."

I said, "Did Sam say anything more to you about getting Claudia to leave?"

Rob rubbed his temples as though I was giving him a headache. "This doesn't have anything to do with Ella's death."

"No," I admitted. But if Sam had a bunch of secrets and Ella found out... "We're just trying to see if we've overlooked anything."

Rob shook his head. "I'm still not sure how Sam's trying to convince Claudia to leave the firm comes into all this."

Neither was I. But I wasn't about to admit that. "How exactly did he try to convince her to leave?"

"Well, he dropped her a hint about a year and a

half ago, something about, wouldn't it be nice if she could just leave the firm and go on a yearlong round-the-world cruise. To which Claudia replied that she'd done without vacations and relationships for so long that it no longer mattered."

"And that was it?"

Rob shrugged. "Sort of. He didn't say anything else to her, but he asked me if I had any ideas for convincing her to leave. I said maybe he could pretend she'd won a yearlong cruise, and she'd take it. I was joking, but he took me seriously."

"He didn't actually do that, did he?"

Rob nodded. "Yep. He got a refundable ticket and mailed it to her, pretending she'd won. Claudia just turned it down."

"Wow."

Rob shrugged. "Yeah, at least he got his money back."

"He was really desperate to get her to leave."

"But don't tell her, okay?" said Rob, his eyes pleading. "I don't want to get caught in the middle of all this."

"Sure," I said, wondering if Claudia suspected that it was Sam who'd gotten her that ticket. "What else did Sam try?"

"Well, when the cruise ticket didn't work, Sam

asked me if I had any other brilliant ideas. I told him that he shouldn't try to mess with her that way. He said it was for her own good—the woman deserved a life."

"And Sam 'deserved' an easier divorce," I snarked.

"Yeah, well, Sam can be convincing. He told me that Claudia often mentioned that she didn't have a well-rounded life. No kids, no boyfriend, no husband, not even any pets."

I felt my chest squeeze tight, and Ian and I exchanged a quick glance. We couldn't imagine life without Snowflake.

"Don't tell me he got her a kitten," said Ian.

"No," said Rob, "he suggested a kitten or a puppy, and I told him that the poor animal would just end up in the pound and I wasn't having any part of it. And then Sam said, what about a boyfriend? As though he could just hand her a boyfriend on a platter."

I frowned. "But she's got a boyfriend now."

"She didn't when Sam and I were having this chat," Rob said. "I told Sam that didn't sound like a good idea, either. And then, next thing you know, we're at this dinner event, and a guy comes up to Sam. The two of them knew each other. Sam introduces him to Claudia, and bingo! They start dating."

"So Sam set the two of them up." Hardly a crime.

"And it lasted," said Rob, leaning back in his chair and looking at us warily. "Claudia and I go way back, and none of her guys last beyond two months. They get sick of her being a workaholic, and I reckon she just doesn't know how to treat a boyfriend."

"Maybe he's the one," Ian suggested.

"Maybe," Rob said slowly, but his eyes had a serious look to them that made me concerned.

"You've met Jarred?" I said.

Rob nodded. "A couple of times."

"And why don't you seem pleased about their relationship?"

Rob shrugged. "I don't know. The whole thing seems a bit off to me. He's so young and good looking—I hope Claudia's not being duped by a gold digger."

Ian and I laughed.

"Claudia seems too smart to be taken in by a gold digger," I said.

"I'm smart," Ian protested. "And you keep saying that I fall for gold diggers."

"You're not smart when it comes to pretty young women," I reminded him.

Rob said, "And maybe Claudia's not being smart enough when it comes to a pretty young man."

I looked at him and smiled gently. "You're concerned for your friend."

Rob shrugged and tried to look tough. "Eh. I just don't think it's fair of Sam to try to push her out of the firm so he can get an easier divorce, and I don't want her getting hurt."

"Speaking of getting hurt," I said, "do you know why she might've left the party early on Friday night?"

"Did she?" Rob's brow creased. "I didn't notice. I'd had a bit to drink that night."

Ian and I exchanged a glance. Maybe Claudia had gone off to meet up with her boyfriend or had just turned in early—or maybe she knew something more about Ella's death.

It was time to go talk to her again.

25

As Ian and I drove toward Toole Springs, Ian's phone rang. I navigated the roads and listened in on his conversation.

"Hi, Nanna," he was saying. "No, I'm not. We're heading north toward Claudia's house, to talk to her. No, I don't know. Sure, why not? I'll text you.

"That was Nanna," he said to me. "She wanted to know if we were home—Gavin stopped by and said he would drop her off at our place. But I told her we're going to Claudia's. So Gavin said he can drop her off at Claudia's, and then we can drive her back with us."

I made a face. "I don't want Nanna meddling in our investigation."

"Gavin said he and Nanna are going to wait in

the car outside. He said he knows you don't want to see him, and he'll make sure not to bother you. Come on, let me text Nanna the address—she won't come inside, and Gavin won't bother you."

"I don't trust Gavin."

"But Nanna's there to make sure he behaves. I'm texting her the address."

I made a face, but I didn't stop him. If Gavin was right that Ian and Nanna were being kept on as the show's "jokers," then perhaps the two of them would make it through to the next round, and they might as well practice their dance routines a little.

We pulled up in front of Claudia's house and strode up to the front door, which she opened within a few minutes of our knock.

"Oh, you two again," she said when she saw us.

She smiled with obviously forced politeness and ushered us in. Today, she was dressed casually in Bermuda shorts and a silky-looking blue top. She wasn't wearing any makeup, but her skin looked creamy and, other than a few crow's-feet near her eyes, absolutely wrinkle-free.

"I'm a bit stressed with a client issue," she told us as we followed her into the living room. "It's been a crazy day."

"You look stressed," Ian said. "Our friend Karma would say that you're giving off stress vibes."

Ian and I sat next to each other on the sofa, and Claudia sat opposite us in a large armchair. Her large leather handbag with files poking out of it lay at her feet, and just as she sat down, her phone buzzed.

"Gotta take this," she said with a sigh as she excused herself and headed out of the room, the phone pressed against her ear.

She was gone for a few minutes, and then we heard footsteps in the hallway. "Yes," Claudia was saying, "no matter what. I will definitely take care of you, no matter where I am."

When she sat down opposite us again, Ian said, "It's amazing how you get any legal work done in between all those phone calls."

Claudia shrugged modestly. "You get used to it, and you learn to work around the calls."

"That's about the third time I've heard you tell someone that you'll take care of them no matter where you are," I said. "What's the deal with that? Are you finally going on vacation?"

Claudia looked at me and frowned. "I don't know what you're talking about."

"You know, you keep saying, 'I'll take care of you

no matter where I go.' Where are you going?"

Claudia shook her head as though she was still confused by my question. "I'm not going anywhere. It's just a figure of speech."

"It does sound like you're going somewhere," Ian insisted. "You're not planning on backpacking through Europe, are you?"

Claudia laughed. "At my age?"

And then it struck me. "You're going to another firm," I said slowly. "You're leaving the offices of Elman and Associates. That's why you keep saying you can take care of your clients wherever you go."

Claudia looked at me, her eyes guarded and unsure. "I'm a partner at Elman and Associates. Why would I go to another firm?"

"Then you're starting your own firm," I said. "Aren't you?"

Ian snapped his fingers and sat up straighter. "That's why you've been missing work events. That's why you work from home so often these days—it's so that you can steal clients away from the other partners."

Claudia glanced from Ian to me as though recognizing she had been backed into a corner. Finally, she shrugged. "All right, I'll admit it—I'm leaving the firm. That's not a crime. What should be a crime is the way those two men are trying to push me out. They think they can cut costs by getting rid of one of the partners—as if that'll help them out."

I thought back to our recent conversation with Rob, and all the tricks Sam had tried. "We've just been talking to Rob. He doesn't want to push you out."

Claudia looked at me hesitantly. "It seemed like they were both in on it."

"Rob told us it was just Sam. He didn't want to encourage Sam—he didn't even realize you knew about Sam's plans."

Claudia rolled her eyes. "Oh, Sam thought he was being so subtle. Giving me hints about yearlong vacations and retiring to marry my boyfriend. They were getting on my nerves, and I knew that pretty soon, they'd call in a partners' vote and try to oust me. It was obvious."

"But Rob didn't seem to want to oust you. Are you sure they *both* wanted you to leave?"

Claudia paused for a moment. "I'm not entirely sure," she admitted. "But Sam needed a divorce, and his buddy Rob would help him get whatever he wanted. The nerve of those two! Trying to push me out of the firm I sacrificed half my life trying to build up. I can't believe—"

"Hang on," Ian said, interrupting her. "How do you know about Sam's divorce?"

Claudia stopped mid-rant and looked at Ian in surprise. "What do you mean?"

"Nobody knows about Sam's affair," Ian said. "It's a big secret."

"It's not such a secret," Claudia said warily. "People know."

"Like who?"

She pressed her lips together, watching Ian steadily.

I said slowly, "Someone must've told you. Keith? No, Keith thought Sam was having an affair with Ella. Ella! That's who told you—she was working closely with Sam, and she must've figured it out somehow."

Claudia looked at me and sighed melodramatically. "Fine. Ella told me about Sam's secret affair. It's not a big deal, everyone would've found out eventually."

"But why did Ella bother to tell you about Sam's affair? Was she trying to help you out?"

"Sort of," said Claudia thinly. "She could tell that the firm was going to come crashing down."

"Crashing down because of Sam's affair?" I said, puzzled.

"You mean because of Sam's spending habits?" suggested Ian.

"Not spending habits," Claudia spat out. "*Embezzlement* habits."

Ian's brows shot up. "Whoa! Sam was embezzling from the firm?"

Claudia looked from me to Ian, and then she shrugged. "What's the harm in telling you? We've come this far. And you're private investigators, you're meant to be discreet. So I might as well tell you— Sam was embezzling funds to reduce the value of the firm, so that when he ultimately did get divorced, he'd have a secret nest egg, and the firm would be worth much less."

"And you're stealing clients, too," I pointed out.

Claudia smiled sweetly. "I only started poaching the clients once I found out about this whole mess."

"Which Ella told you about," I said slowly. So this was the secret Ella had told her friend Felicity about.

Claudia nodded. "Yes."

"And what would have happened to Ella once the firm split up?"

"She was going to come with me to my new firm," said Claudia. "She was a smart kid. I promised to fast-track her to partner for all the information she was getting me."

"So she really did look up to you as a mentor."

Something flashed in Claudia's eyes, but I couldn't place what it was. Anger? But she had no reason to be angry.

But whatever it was died out and her eyes looked sad again. "Poor Ella. I didn't want her to think of me as her mentor. Look at me—I'm old and I don't really have the life I want. No relationships, no vacations, and the partners are trying to kick me out of my own firm."

"You do have a relationship," Ian reminded her. "Dancing Jarred."

Claudia laughed, but there wasn't much humor in her eyes. "Sure."

Something about her attitude toward her relationship seemed off. Even when I'd been unsure about a boyfriend, I'd never completely forgotten that I was in a relationship. I said slowly, "Sam was the one who introduced you to Jarred. And he'd been hoping you two would get married, and then you'd leave the firm."

"But that didn't happen," said Ian. "I guess you didn't like Jarred as much as Sam thought you would."

"I like him enough," Claudia said mildly. "Now, did you two have anything else you wanted to talk about?"

But Ian wasn't done. "There was something special about Jarred," he said. "Rob told us most of your relationships ended after two months. And Sam did tell Rob that he'd get you a nice boyfriend to keep you busy."

Claudia's eyes narrowed and she said through gritted teeth, "He said *what* to Rob?!"

I looked at her carefully. "That he'd get you a boyfriend. A boyfriend who's stuck around much longer than anyone expected."

"Sam's paying Jarred," Ian said suddenly. "Jarred's an actor. Sam's paying Jarred to act the part of your boyfriend."

Claudia's eyes were glittering with rage, and she opened her mouth to say something and then closed it again. Finally, she said, "This is ridiculous! How dare you insult me and my boyfriend?"

I watched her carefully. "It's not really an insult. We're just wondering what if..."

"You must think I'm some foolish old lady," snapped Claudia, her rage not abating, her face starting to go red.

"No," Ian and I chimed in unison.

Ian said, "I'll bet Ella was the one who told you about Jarred's being paid by Sam."

Claudia didn't say anything, but she shook her head no and took a few deep breaths, trying to calm herself down.

"Maybe Jarred had something to do with Ella's death," I said, thinking out loud. "He didn't want Ella to tell you the truth, then when he found out that she already had, he killed her."

"We should go talk to Jarred," said Ian. "See if he'll admit to killing Ella."

"No," said Claudia suddenly. "Leave him out of this."

We looked at her in surprise.

"I know you must still like him," I said, "but he might be a killer."

"He's not," said Claudia, her voice suddenly tinged with desperation. "You have to leave this alone."

I shook my head. "How can you be so sure he's not a killer? You might be in danger yourself. Besides, we're pretty sure Sam just hired him to act like your boyfriend."

Claudia's eyes watched Ian and me carefully, the rage draining out of them. "That's not true," she said.

She twisted a strand of her dark hair, and I felt a pang of sympathy for her.

"You've had a tough time," I said. "And maybe Sam hired Jarred initially, but now he loves you." I didn't believe the words even as I said them, but I wanted to cheer Claudia up a bit. She was gazing off into space, and her eyes looked glazed over.

"No," Claudia said. "No, no. This isn't happening. Not now. Not again."

"What do you mean, again?"

But Claudia just muttered to herself and continued to twist her hair. She looked nothing like the self-confident lawyer she'd been a minute ago, and I wondered what had happened to her. All her anger had drained out, replaced by what seemed to be fear and shock.

"It's ok," Ian said, reassuringly. "We won't tell anyone. Even if it does turn out that Jarred was an actor. He probably was, and he probably never loved you." Ian was nothing if not diplomatic. "It makes sense that Sam hired an actor to try to get you out of the way."

Claudia looked at Ian with wide eyes, and I said quickly, "Even if he really does love you, it's best to be safe. He might be a killer."

Claudia turned to look at me, and shook her

head disbelievingly. She seemed to be in shock, and Ian and I exchanged a glance.

After a long silence, Claudia said, "You two are right. Jarred *was* hired by Sam. But Sam stopped paying him six months ago. He really does love me."

"Did you check his bank accounts?" I said.

Claudia shook her head. "No, I trust him."

"Well, we don't," said Ian bluntly. "We'll have to look into him."

"Fine," said Claudia faintly, "do what you have to. But Jarred had nothing to do with it. You won't learn anything, so it doesn't matter if you talk to him."

"You seem awfully sure that Jarred had nothing to do with Ella's death," I said slowly. "Which means that you know something more."

Claudia looked at me, her eyes glinting, and I could tell she was hiding something.

"You don't have to protect Jarred," Ian said. "Just tell us the truth."

Claudia shrugged. "I've told you everything. I don't want you to bother Jarred, but I can't stop you if you really want to."

She stood up, as though to show us out, and then I remembered why we'd come here in the first place.

"Where were you on the Friday night Ella was killed?" I said.

Claudia looked at me sharply. "I already told you, at that office party."

"No," I said. "You left early."

Claudia sat down slowly, and frowned. "Really? I must've forgotten."

I waited for her to think, and then finally, she shrugged. "I must've come home early for some reason. I don't remember doing anything else that night."

"So you didn't drive over to see Ella?"

"No."

Something in her eyes told me she was lying. So taking a stab in the dark, I said, "I think you did go to see her. In fact, I think you killed her. And I think Jarred's got something to do with it."

Claudia laughed drily. "Why would I kill her after all that girl did for me?"

"I don't know," I admitted. "But I'm sure, if we show photos of your car to Ella's neighbors, they'll recognize it."

"It's a generic Mazda," said Claudia. "None of the neighbors would remember it."

We stared at her, shocked, and then Claudia realized what she'd said.

Before we knew it, Claudia had bent down, reached into the handbag sitting on the floor next to her, and pulled out a small but deadly-looking handgun.

She pointed it at me and said, "I think we've done enough talking for today."

26

I froze. My mouth felt dry, and I wasn't sure what to say. Finally, I gulped and said, "That's okay, we don't need to talk about it anymore. You don't need to have that gun out."

"I think I do," Claudia said. She swiveled the gun from me to Ian, then back to me again. "I knew the cops would think it was a mugging, just a general 'bad neighborhood' crime. Then you two came along—I thought you were amateurs, but you just kept poking and poking..."

Her voice trailed off, and beside me, I could feel the fear emanating from Ian. Claudia had killed once, which meant she wouldn't hesitate to kill again. What did she intend to do with us? Maybe she wasn't sure herself. Maybe I could stop her from killing us if I just acted a bit sympathetic.

I tried to look understanding and forced myself to say kindly, "Why don't you tell us what happened? It must've been a very difficult situation for you, with the firm and Jarred and everything happening at once."

Claudia sighed and looked at me. The faint, unnoticeable lines in her face seemed etched deeper, and her eyes looked tired. "It was all Sam's fault. He's the one who's the real criminal, not me. Embezzling from the firm, paying a man to act like my boyfriend, trying to push me out... he forced me to snap."

I nodded. "What a horrible, horrible man."

"Exactly. And if it hadn't been for Ella, I wouldn't even have known."

"Then why kill Ella?" I said. "She was your friend."

Claudia's eyes dropped to the floor for a split second, and I wondered if she was upset and could be overpowered. But in the next instant, she looked back at me again, the gun in her hand not wavering.

"I was wrong," Claudia said softly. "I was wrong about Ella."

I waited for her to go on, and when she didn't, I said, "You thought she wasn't your friend."

Claudia took a deep breath and nodded. "It feels

good to get this off my chest. I never thought I could keep it a secret, but once I tell you guys everything and then get rid of you, I'll have shared everything, and my secret will still be safe."

A chill ran down my spine and I pressed my hands together to stop them from shaking. She had it all planned out. I wasn't going to make her feel sorry for us and let us go, but I needed to buy some time to figure out what to do. No way was I going to die at the hands of some maniacal lawyer. Beside me, Ian let out a soft whimper of fear. I forced myself to sound calm and said, "Yes, it's a good idea to share what happened. You'll feel much better."

Claudia nodded. "I'm starting to feel better already. You see, the whole thing was a mistake. Ella told me about the embezzling and the move to push me out of the firm, and I was grateful. But then I thought, maybe she's taking advantage of me. On the night of the dinner, she called me to say she had learned something new."

"So you picked her up from her apartment."

"Yes, and she told me that Jarred was actually an actor hired by Sam to seduce me away from the firm. She'd heard Sam laughing to Rob that I was a silly, love-starved middle-aged woman."

Claudia fell silent, and I prompted her, "And you didn't like that."

"No," said Claudia vehemently. "I didn't, and I didn't believe it. I was furious. I accused Ella of trying to manipulate me, trying to get more out of me than she deserved. I was driving her home and made a detour to Balzar Avenue, where I told her to get out of the car. I just wanted to scare her, wanted her to have to find her own way home late at night from Balzar."

"Wow," I said, unable to help myself. That was pretty cruel. "What did she do?"

"She refused to get out of my car," Claudia said, her voice rising an octave. "I needed to think about what she'd said, and the girl stopped cooperating with me. I pulled out my gun, just to get her to leave the car, and then when we were out, she told me she'd changed her mind, she wouldn't come to my new firm, and she'd press charges against me for assault. She turned and started walking away, and that's when I snapped. My life was crumbling, this girl was using me and now she'd claim I'd assaulted her—it was too much. I yelled something at her, telling her off, and when she turned around to look at me, I did it. I pulled the trigger before I knew what I was doing."

There was silence for a few seconds. And then, Claudia said, "I didn't really mean to kill her. I just saw red... and then, afterward, I found out she was telling the truth about Jarred. Men. That's the issue. They use you and get you in trouble."

"But you're not a man," Ian said, sounding terrified.

"No," snapped Claudia, "I'm a victim of fate."

I nodded, trying to look like I felt sorry for her. What was it with people who always pretended to be a victim? She was wealthy, successful, and well-respected as a lawyer. So what if her life wasn't perfect? Nobody's life was perfect. Didn't mean they had to go around killing people.

"It's so tough," I murmured, trying to sound like I empathized with her.

"It is," Claudia said. She glanced from Ian to me and stood up. Her brows knit, and her eyes narrowed. "And now, I have to get rid of you."

My heart jumped into my throat, and my breath was short and jagged.

I had to think fast. I needed some way to distract Claudia. Perhaps I could make a wild dash for her gun and overpower her, but if I moved toward her, she'd shoot me. Perhaps I could trick her somehow, or convince her that Ian and I would keep her secret.

But Claudia seemed too smart for trickery or false promises.

"You don't need to get rid of us," I heard myself saying. "I'm sure we could come to some understanding."

"I know your type," said Claudia, her voice like steel. "You think you're oh-so-good and better than the rest of us. Well, you're not, and you're not getting me in trouble. I've gotten away with one murder, and I know that getting rid of you two will be easy."

Just then, there was a loud knock at Claudia's door.

Claudia stiffened and glared at us. "Don't make a noise," she hissed. "Whoever it is will go away."

The knocking continued for a few long minutes, and then finally, there was silence. A few seconds later, Ian's phone began to ring.

"I'd better answer that," Ian said quickly. "It's probably my mother, and she'll get all worried if I don't answer."

"I'm not stupid," Claudia snapped. "You're not answering any phone calls."

We waited until Ian's cell phone stopped ringing, and then Claudia turned to me. She opened her mouth to say something, when my phone began to ring.

I knew what her answer would be, so I didn't bother to ask Claudia if I could answer. Instead, I used the time that my phone was ringing to wonder if I should rush over and try to overpower her. But I was sitting down, and if I got up suddenly, Claudia would get suspicious.

When my phone stopped ringing, the knocking at the door started again.

And then, I heard Nanna's voice saying, "Open up! I know you guys are in there."

27

My heart plunged to my knees. What was Nanna doing here? Gavin had promised that he and Nanna would wait in the car, a fact that I had completely forgotten about.

"I saw your car parked out there," Nanna's voice continued after a pause. "Gavin says he has to rush off, so I need to wait inside with you two."

I kicked myself for ever trusting Gavin.

Of course he would be the flakiest, most unreliable person in the world. And now, Nanna would have to get mixed up in all this.

A wave of fear and anger washed over me. I closed my eyes, wishing this were all just a terrible dream.

There was silence for a few seconds, and I was

hopeful that perhaps Nanna and Gavin had walked away. I opened my eyes weakly and saw that Claudia was still pointing the gun at me. She looked angrier than ever and was glaring at me as though the knocking on her door was all my fault. Which, in a way, it was.

"Tiffany," Nanna's voice said again, "do you want your nanna to stand out here in the street?"

"Who's that?" Claudia said to me. "Who is this woman?"

"It's my nanna," I said, feeling helpless.

Claudia looked at me like I was stupid. "Your nanna?"

"She was supposed to wait outside in Gavin's car." I knew none of what I said made sense, and I needed to get Nanna away from Claudia's house. "She's just an old woman. She can't be standing out in the sun and heat all by herself."

The insistent knocking started again, and Ian's cell phone buzzed.

"It's Nanna who's been calling all this time," Ian said.

Claudia scowled darkly. "Don't answer. If she thinks no one's home, she'll go away."

I laughed, despite the chilling hands of fear squeezing tight around my chest. "You don't know my nanna. She's going to stand out there and knock and knock until all your neighbors come out and ask you what's going on."

Claudia let out an exasperated grunt. "We need her to go away."

I nodded rapidly. "I agree, I don't want her coming in."

"Tell her to get a taxi or something."

I shook my head. "I don't think that will work—she won't want to wait outside in the heat while she knows that she could wait in here with us." And then, a brainwave struck. "Why don't I give her my car keys, and she can wait outside in my car while she waits for a taxi to arrive?"

Claudia turned the idea over in her mind.

The knocking started again, and this time, I heard Gavin's voice saying, "Tiffany, hurry up, I really need to rush off. I've got a work emergency."

Claudia sighed, as though she could imagine all her neighbors running out to see what the commotion was about.

"Fine," she said, sounding grumpy and reluctant. "Here's what we'll do. You'll go open the door, and I'll stand behind you, pointing this gun at your back. You'll give your Nanna your bag, and you'll tell her to take your keys and wait in your car. If you try anything funny, I'll kill you, and then I'll kill your nanna."

I nodded rapidly, trying not to hear the loud thudding in my chest. "Agreed."

"Stay where you are," Claudia said to Ian. "Don't try anything stupid, or your friend here gets it."

Ian nodded quickly. "Yes, exactly. No, I mean, no. Of course I won't do anything stupid. I'll just sit here. I can't even think of anything stupid to do. I mean, I'll just sit here. I won't do anything."

Claudia stared at Ian skeptically for a few seconds, trying to decide if she believed his scared act, or if he was some kind of deceptive superhero who would jump up the minute her back was turned and wrench the gun out of her hands. In the end, she decided that with Ian, what you saw was what you got—there was no way he could save the day.

"Pick up your bag and walk over to the door," Claudia said to me. "Remember, no funny business."

I did as she said. All I wanted to do was give Nanna the bag and have her wait for me in the car. Once Nanna was far away from Claudia, I could try to figure out a plan. Claudia positioned herself behind me so that anyone standing in front of me wouldn't be able to see the gun.

We opened the door just as Nanna had raised her hand to knock again.

"It took you long enough!" Nanna said. She was wearing tan slacks and a floral-print blouse, and she looked flushed from standing in the midday sun for too long. "Gavin here's decided to run off and abandon me."

I glared at Gavin disapprovingly. This was all his fault.

Claudia was standing a foot behind me, and I could sense the gun pointed at my back.

Nanna looked at Claudia and said, "Who're you?"

"This is Claudia," I said quickly. "We were just having a quick chat." I didn't want to waste time berating Gavin, so I handed Nanna my bag and said, "My car keys are in there. Go wait for me in the car, and I'll come join you when I'm done."

"Don't be silly," Nanna said. "Why should I wait for you in the car?"

"We're having a private conversation here," I said. "I really need you to go and wait for me in the car."

I motioned with my head toward my car, and gave her a desperate look. I hoped she would get the hint, and for once, stay out of trouble.

Instead, Nanna said, "I need to come in and see Ian. I've just had a brilliant idea for a dance routine."

"You can tell him when we're done talking to Claudia," I said slowly. "Please. Just go and wait for me in the car."

"I can't do that," Nanna said. "I need to see Ian *right now* and show him the routine. Otherwise I'll forget."

From behind me, Claudia said, "I can't let you into the house. There are some issues with the flooring, and I don't want you to get hurt."

"Don't be silly," Nanna said. "I'm not that old. I'm not about to hurt myself. I'll just show Ian this dance routine, and then I'll go do what she said, go wait in the car. It'll just be a couple of seconds."

I turned back to look at Claudia. I really didn't know what to do—Nanna wasn't about to give up without showing Ian her new brainwave of a dance routine. On the other hand, maybe she could just come inside and talk to Ian for a few seconds, and he would convince her to wait in the car.

Claudia rolled her eyes and took a large step toward me.

She grabbed my left arm tightly with her hand and pressed the gun into the small of my back.

She stood close enough to me that nobody would be able to see the gun. If she chose to, she could fire off a bullet that would leave me paralyzed or dead.

"Come in," Claudia said to Nanna. I could feel the chill emanating from her. "Show Ian your dance routine, and then go wait in the car for Tiffany."

My palms were clammy. Nanna handed my bag back to me. She smiled cheerfully, ignorant of the real situation.

"That's more like it!" she said happily. "I know this routine I've just thought of is brilliant, and it'll definitely get us through to the next round."

"I want to see this routine of yours," Gavin said, quickly following Nanna inside.

"I thought you had to run off to work." I glared at him furiously. "That's why you tried to dump Nanna in the middle of the street."

"Don't be so dramatic," Gavin said. "Don't you want me to help your nanna and Ian get through to the next round?"

Nanna and Gavin headed into the living room while Claudia and I stood in the foyer, looking in through the living room doorway.

Claudia kept her grip on my arm, and the gun pressed against the small of my back. I could feel its steely presence, poking against me in a constant reminder of the danger I was in. Ian shot me a panicked look, and I twisted my lips, trying to indicate that I didn't know what to do.

Gavin plonked himself down onto one of the dark leather sofas and crossed his legs, leaning back to watch the show.

"I've thought of this really cool move I can do when you do your twerking," Nanna said. "Instead of just moving my hands in front of my face, I can do something different. Let's practice it now—you do your twerking, and I'll do my move."

"But I don't have any music," Ian said desperately.

"Just practice your move," said Claudia, through clenched teeth. "Do your dance thing, and then the two of them can get out of here."

"Put the music on your phone," said Nanna. "You've got a track on there, don't you?"

Ian looked to Claudia, wordlessly asking her what to do.

"Play the music," hissed Claudia, her fingers digging sharply into my arm.

Ian fished out his phone. His hands trembled as

he turned the playlist on. The music started pumping out, and the fast, upbeat tune made me feel like I was in some kind of horrific madhouse.

Ian stood up nervously and walked to the middle of the living room floor, two feet away from where Nanna was standing.

He looked at me, his eyes wild with fear and apprehension, and I glanced away. I didn't want Claudia to get spooked by anything. The gun poking into my back was a reminder that I needed to stay calm. I needed Nanna to show us her dance brainwave and then leave. Safely, and in one piece.

Ian and Nanna stood there awkwardly while the music played. When the twerking section of the song started, Ian dropped down into a low squat and began moving his hips and twerking furiously.

Immediately, Nanna started throwing her hands up into the air, as though she was some kind of geriatric cheerleader. She seemed to be holding invisible pom-poms in her hands, and she waved them first one way, then the other. The two of them looked completely ridiculous.

For a brief moment, I forgot all about Claudia and the gun that was digging into my back. My jaw dropped. Gavin burst out laughing, and I heard Claudia say under her breath, "Whoa."

The fingers gripping my arm seemed to have loosened their grip a little.

The fog of fear clouding my brain appeared to lift. Realization struck: Claudia must've been staring at Ian and Nanna, as bug-eyed and shocked as I'd been the first time I'd seen their routine.

I didn't hesitate.

I spun around and gripped Claudia's gun hand, twisting her arm to the side so she was pointing the gun away from the living room, and toward the door that I assumed was the garage door. Using all my strength, I shoved her down onto the floor and knelt over her.

Claudia clawed at me. My sudden move had caught her off guard. She fired a bullet into the garage door, and then another. She pressed her arm up, trying to point the gun back at me, and I leaned against her, using all my force to hold her arm in place.

Loud footsteps raced toward me, and then Ian was by my side. He helped me hold Claudia down, and somehow, I managed to wrench the gun from Claudia's hand.

I handed the gun to Ian, and he pointed it at Claudia.

"Stay on the floor," he said.

"What about our dance routine?" I heard Nanna saying from the living room. She sounded confused and disappointed. "What's going on? If we don't practice, I'm going to forget everything."

I stood up shakily, and Claudia glared at me. "You and your dance routines," she hissed. "I should never have let them dance in here."

"You should never have done a lot of things," I said. "You should never have killed Ella, and you should never have tried to kill Ian and me."

28

Claudia stared at us with silent, angry eyes until the cops arrived.

The two young officers who showed up knew me from one of my previous cases. They listened to my story carefully, handcuffed Claudia, and led her away.

"You all need to stop by the station today," one of them said to us. "We'll need official statements from all of you."

After they drove off, Ian, Nanna, Gavin and I stood in front of Claudia's house and shuffled our feet, not wanting to leave.

The fear and adrenaline I'd felt when Claudia had threatened to kill Ian and me, and then Nanna, was starting to wear off. Exhaustion began seeping into my veins. I knew I needed to go home and rest, but I also couldn't wait to talk to Ella's sister and tell her that I'd solved the case.

"That was quite interesting," Gavin was saying. "I didn't know being an investigator could be so interesting. If I'd known, I wouldn't have told you to stop."

The sun was beating down, and I was starting to feel like it was time to get out of the heat and maybe go somewhere that was cool and peaceful. Maybe it was time to close my eyes and have a nice long nap.

"When did you tell me to stop investigating?" I said distractedly. It must've been when he'd been randomly chatting over lunch at my parents' house, and I probably hadn't paid attention.

"I sent you that note, remember? I thought that if you'd stop investigating this case, maybe we could spend more time together, or maybe you'd help Ian and Nanna with their reality TV show thing, and then you'd want to be nice to me."

I turned to Gavin and frowned. A prickle of apprehension was crawling up my spine, and I said, "What note?"

"You know, the note I sent you," Gavin said. "I said to stop investigating, ha ha. I added the 'ha ha' so that you'd know it was a joke."

My chest tightened with a flash of anger. I saw a

blinding, bright light that made it hard to focus. My breath was hot and angry, and my temples began to throb.

"You left that note?" Ian was saying. "That was a really stupid thing to do. We could've had you arrested for harassment."

I focused all my energies on breathing deeply and staying calm. My fingers curled into fists and uncurled. I needed to stop myself from jumping at Gavin and trying to strangle him.

How could someone be such an idiot? I had been afraid for my life, sure that a psychopathic killer was on our trail—that last part about the psychopathic killer had kind of been true, but I didn't need an irresponsible person like Gavin sending me "joke" death threats.

"Whoa," Gavin was saying. "It was a joke. I'm sure Tiffany can take a joke."

I took a deep breath and tried to steady myself. "Ian's right," I said. "That was a stupid thing to do, and I'll be glad if I never see you again."

I marched off, not hearing whatever Gavin was saying in reply. If I stayed near him another second, I would soon be the one accused of murder, and I didn't want that to happen.

Ian and Nanna followed me to my car, and as we

drove off, Nanna said, "He seemed like such a nice young man. But at least he's just silly and not really dangerous."

"Silly people can be dangerous," I said. "They just don't know it."

I hoped I would never have to see Gavin again, but somehow, I doubted it.

29

A few days later, I was at the casino, dealing out cards to blackjack players, smiling and chatting with them as they won and lost their hands.

The chime of a jackpot siren went off from one of the slot machines, and I heard an excited scream, followed by loud laughter.

"Seems like the slot machines are more fun than blackjack," one of the players sitting opposite me said wryly.

I knew he was joking, so I said, "It depends on your game. I know poker players who hate slot machines."

We chatted for a minute about different games, and when the conversation ran out and the players focused on their game, I let my thoughts drift off to the dinner I'd just had with Ryan.

I'd told him about Gavin and his stupid prank and asked, "Can't you arrest him for something? Harassment, or general stupidity?"

Ryan had laughed, a deep belly laugh that made his gray eyes crinkle up, and made me smile.

"I'm afraid not," he'd said. "The man admitted to what he'd done, and though it wasn't funny at all, there's nothing we can do about it."

I'd changed the topic and tried to forget about Gavin, chatting instead about how crazy Claudia had turned out to be. Ryan told me that Claudia had lawyered up, but given her confession and attempt on our lives, it was unlikely she'd be able to avoid justice.

THE NEXT MORNING, there was a loud knock on my door just after noon.

I opened it to find Ian standing in the hallway with Snowflake under his arm, his face positively radiating with excitement.

"I have excellent news," he said, rushing into my apartment and setting Snowflake down on the floor.

Snowflake immediately raced to the top of the fridge, where she sat down, licked her paws, and stared down at the two of us superciliously.

"What is it?" I said warily. All too often, Ian's excellent news doesn't sound particularly excellent to me.

"The producers of *Dance Party USA* contacted me and Nanna," he said, his voice brimming with enthusiasm. "We didn't get through to the next round!"

I frowned. "I thought you wanted to get through. You're excited about this?"

Ian shook his head. "No, no, it's tragic we didn't get in and all that. But the good news is, they were so impressed by my performance, they want me to appear on another reality TV show! It's some kind of survival show. They looked me up in that audition we did for that singing show, and they said that I've got talent. They want me to appear on TV! Isn't that wonderful? I'm going to audition for the show next week, and then I can be one of the contestants!"

I looked at Ian hesitantly. I wasn't convinced that his appearing on another reality TV show was a good idea. I didn't want to dampen his enthusiasm either, so I said, "That might be fun for you. I hope I don't need to get involved with the show or anything."

"No, you don't. I just have to spend a few hours taping the show, and that's it! It's going to be so much fun!"

I nodded, not entirely convinced. I wanted Ian to have fun, but my experience of his adventures has been that he often gets into trouble, and I'm forced to bail him out.

I had a bad feeling about Ian's plans for the reality TV show, but I smiled and tried to look supportive.

"I'll be along for the ride," I said, with forced cheerfulness.

Of course, I didn't know just what that ride would entail.

JOIN THE AR WINTERS NEWSLETTER

∾

Find out about the latest releases by AR Winters,
and get access to exclusive free copies of her books:

Click Here To Join

You can also follow AR Winters on Facebook

Made in the USA
Coppell, TX
08 April 2021